WHEN WE WERE GOOD

Published in 2013 by Sumach Press, an imprint of Three O'Clock Press Inc.
425 Adelaide St. W. #200 | Toronto ON | M5V3C1
www.threeoclockpress.com

Library and Archives Canada Cataloguing in Publication

Sutherland, Suzanne, 1987-   When we were good / Suzanne Sutherland.

ISBN 978-1-927513-11-8

I. Title.

PS8637.U865W44 2013   jC813'.6   C2013-901760-7

Printed and bound in Canada by Marquis

Three O'Clock Press gratefully acknowledges the support of the Canada Council
for the Arts, the Ontario Arts Council, and the Department of Canadian
Heritage through the Canada Book Fund.

For Gramma

1

There was a wall of air, of wind, and the noise was everywhere all at once, like a choir of horns, like a chorus of howls. It was louder than I ever thought a sound could be—even more shrill than the wail of the Kathedral's wall of sound—and it swallowed me whole. I reached out, grabbing blind. Crouching between the rails, I swept my arm across the track to feel for what I'd lost, which was everything, my eyes clamped shut in terror.

But it was nowhere. The taunting smile, which I'd seen only seconds before, was gone. There was nothing. Nothing, and the headlights bearing down on me, their glare so strong I could see my blood pulsing in the veins behind my eyelids.

I hurled my body under the lip of the platform just as the driver threw the emergency brake on the train and it squealed to a stop in front of where I lay, fetal and dazed. The stink of steel as the train dragged on the rails filled my head with fire and made my eyes water. I felt my breath stuck in my throat like a piece of hard candy and coughed hard, gulping air. The subway doors opened and I heard five heavy, hurried steps coming toward me.

"Can you hear me? Are you all right down there?" a voice said.

"N-n-no. Y-yes. I-I'm not, I'm not huh-hurt or anything, but-but-but my chest is too tight? It's like I c-c-can't breathe."

"Okay. Just stay calm, all right? Stay still, don't try to move. Stay still. We're going to get you out of here, all right? What's your name?"

"K-Katherine B-b-Boat-m-man."

"You're going to be okay, Katherine. You're going to be all right."

"Oh-huh-oh-kay."

The train was stopped. He'd stopped it, the driver. He'd stopped the train because of me, because I was just lying there, because I couldn't find it, because the answer to everything was gone. It stopped, the train, with all the people in it. I stopped everyone. They were stuck because of me.

They made an announcement saying, "All passengers please leave the train, all passengers, please leave the train." And then I heard more voices, I couldn't tell how many, asking how long the delay would be and complaining that they had to get home to their kids. Some of the voices were mad at me, but some blamed the other people on the subway platform for not trying to stop me.

And then there were paramedics and police. "You had a panic attack," a professionally calm woman in a uniform told me, "from the shock of the train coming at you. But why were you down on the tracks in the first place? How could anything be so bad that you thought it was worth it?"

"I-I didn't," I said, "I didn't think. I didn't-I didn't want to die."

"So why, then? Why did you do it?"

There were three reasons, really: Marie's bitter, crushing disappointment; Megan's laughter—that cruel sneer; and Grandma's last feeble breaths. But I couldn't tell her. I couldn't make my mouth form the words.

2

The beginning was bad. The start of the new year, New Year's Eve. To everyone else it seemed like a miracle that the world hadn't come to an end. It was the year 2000 and everything, Y2K, but all those news reports that told us we should be stockpiling bottled water and canned food turned out to be just another fake scare. The computers figured it all out, and there we were, the same place we'd been in 1999. Only I didn't have a grandmother anymore.

She died during our big family New Year's Eve party. It was awful. While every other person in the world with a television was watching a ball drop and kissing each other and blowing their noisemakers, we were watching Grandma get loaded onto a stretcher in the living room. It was a heart attack, they said, the paramedics in their cargo pants. But she didn't go clutching her chest and moaning and making a big scene. She was graceful, like always, and then she was gone.

We rode to the hospital through streets crowded with people who were, miraculously, all still alive. And Grandma died two days later.

It was a horrible way to start the new year. With the woman who'd pretty much raised me gone, I was in a really bad place. Which is a phrase I've heard so many times that I know it's a cliché, but when your sadness becomes such a constant, heavy part of your life—this blanket laid over top of everything else that smothers anything good so that you're totally blocked off from every other person in the world—your sadness is the bad place. And you can't remember it ever being another way.

I couldn't remember how safe and secure I felt when I was with Grandma. How everything I said seemed important when she was the one listening to me. I couldn't remember the slow, dawning smile that would take over her face when she found me standing on her doorstep, come to visit, to play cards and eat Swiss cheese and avocado on crackers. I couldn't remember the wonderful things she told me I was: smart and kind and beautiful. All I could think of was that I would never feel her arms—strong, and then weaker as she got older and so did I—wrapped around me again, breathing in her sweet smell of peppermint and Yardley's Lavender.

I had a week or so from the end of the world until school

started again. Mom was channelling her grief over her mother's death into work and funeral planning, and Dad was in the middle of some big trade or merger or whatever and was home even less than usual. I don't get my parents' marriage at all. They've been together forever—they met when they were in university—but they have absolutely nothing in common, apart from being superhumanly driven in their careers. I asked my mom once, in a weirdly candid moment after she'd had a couple of glasses of wine, how she knew that Dad was the one when he proposed to her the summer after they graduated. She told me that she didn't, that she had just hoped for the best. What does that say about hope, about anything?

So I was alone in the house, pretty much just crying and reading Grandma's old books and trying to keep some part of her alive inside of me. In four days I read almost everything Alice Munro had ever written. She was Grandma's favourite; her short stories were these perfect little pearl worlds that lured me out of my own head for the few hours that I gave myself over to them completely. I fell asleep more than once face down in Grandma's old hardcover copy of Munro's *Selected Stories*, long after the words had stopped making sense.

I remembered, vividly, visiting Grandma at her old

house—the one she lived in with my grandpa, who died before I was born; the one she lived in before she moved into the old folks' home when I was fifteen, when Mom wouldn't let her come live with us. She'd play with me all day and she'd never lose her patience the way my parents always seemed to. And when we were finished playing, when I was finally exhausted from our imaginary trips to the Sahara and the Amazon, she'd tell me it was time for our books, and we'd sit together in her living room, me with some dumb Baby-Sitter's Club book and her with Alice Munro or Margaret Atwood or Jane Urquhart, with a little glass candy dish filled with scotch mints between us. I'd fill my pockets up with the candies before I left, and she'd pretend not to notice. On the ride home with Mom, or sometimes Dad, I'd stuff the mints into my mouth one by one, trying hard to just suck on them, but giving in and biting down hard, the candies' granular coolness filling my mouth.

Those were perfect days. But there wouldn't be any more of those.

I spent an entire afternoon lying in the bathtub, staring at the sink's leaky faucet, willing it to stop dripping. Each drop that landed in the basin with a dull plunk was laughing at me and my desperation to feel like I had control over anything.

The water turned cold around me, but I stayed there, shivering, well into the evening.

By the fifth day, there was nothing edible left in the fridge apart from a stick of unsalted butter and some unmarked leftovers, fuzzy with mould. Apparently Mom and Dad were simply too busy to pick up some groceries—this wasn't exactly a new development, our phone had five different take-out places on speed dial—so I finally had to leave the house. I took Mom's credit card from her purse on the kitchen counter, put on my boots and my coat, and left.

I expected the neighbourhood to look different after spending the better part of a week in voluntary confinement, but the salty sidewalks and snow that barely covered the grey grass looked the same. And it was sunny, really sunny. I couldn't believe how bright it was, the sun stung my eyes. I tucked my head down and stared at the sidewalk and my feet as I resignedly put one in front of the other, in front of the other, in front of the other.

I found my way to the grocery store and loaded up a basket with whatever packages I recognized: the cereal Dad likes when he's around the house long enough to eat breakfast, the crackers Mom buys when she's expecting guests, the peanut butter I brought to school every day with honey or banana or strawberry jam between slices of white bread with the crusts cut off when I was a kid. I wanted anything familiar.

I got in line behind an elderly woman with three bananas and a carton of milk. I wanted to tell her that she could take the short line, the express lane, but she was wearing a red wool coat like Grandma's and my face got all tight like it does right before I'm about to cry and instead I ducked back into the frozen food aisle, took a package of blueberry frozen waffles out of the freezer and read the ingredients list line by line.

By the time I was finished, the woman in the red coat had paid for her food and left the store. I lined up again, paid with Mom's Visa and started walking back home.

At Brunswick and Bloor I rested my bags on the sidewalk. As I was about to cross to the north side of the street, I paused, picked up my bags and waddled into Book City instead. I blocked the doorway, coming in with all the groceries, and a young couple with a baby in a stroller looked annoyed, waiting for me to get out of their way. The security fences went off as I walked through them, and while I struggled to get out of the way and explain that I wasn't stealing anything, one of my bags split open and a box of Life cereal and two bags of barbeque chips hit the floor. One of the girls behind the cash gave me a pitying look and came around to help me clean up the mess, saying, "Don't worry about it, it happens!" while she got me a new bag and helped stash my stuff behind the counter.

I mumbled "Thank you," trying to hide my eyes as my face started getting tight again, and walked toward the back of the store, stopping at the kids section.

I spent a long time there, just browsing, trying to remember books I'd loved when I was little. I sat on a stool by the picture books reading Robert Munsch for a while, but then a little boy came by, holding his dad's hand. They saw me sitting there, crying quietly and turning the pages too fast, and then the little boy started crying and his dad looked totally helpless, so I got up to leave, fast. I'd just pushed the door open to go when the girl who'd helped me out before yelled, "Hey, don't forget your groceries!" I turned around, my face completely red and still trying to hide the fact that I'd been crying, and noticed that someone had dropped a bill on the ground. I picked it up. Red, a fifty. Not wanting to draw attention to myself, I passed it off to the clerk who'd been nice to me.

"I found this on the ground," I said, "over there by the

door. Did you maybe drop it from the till or something?"

"Oh, wow," she said. "No, I don't think so." She held the money up in the air and called out, "Did anybody lose a fifty?"

A few people who were looking at the shelves nearby chuckled. "Geez," someone said, "I wish I had fifty bucks to lose."

"Looks like it's yours now," the girl said. "Must be your lucky day."

"I really don't think I should take it."

A man standing behind me spoke up. "Take it," he said. "Do something good."

The clerk passed me my groceries over the counter, then handed the bill back to me. "He's right," she said, "you could do a lot of good with that money."

I made a weak smile, then folded the bill and put it in my coat pocket. "Sure," I said, "something good. I'll try."

When I got home Mom was in the kitchen, on the phone with one of her producers. She kept on talking, while I put away the groceries. When I finally managed to get the freezer door to close—stuffed as it was with ice cream, waffles, mac and cheese, and curly fries—she hung up.

"Thanks, honey," she said. "What a big help. So... helpful."

"Yeah, it's no problem. I mean, we still have to eat, right? I used your card, by the way. Here you go," I said, handing her the Visa.

"Terrific. Great. Yes. Of course. We still have to..." she was talking in her not-all-there way.

"What?" I said, trying to snap her out of it.

"Huh? Oh. Dinner, we need to have dinner. I was hoping we could all eat together tonight."

"Is Dad coming home early?"

"I'm still waiting to hear from him. If his meeting's on tonight or not. We could still eat, though. The two of us. We could eat."

"I'm not really hungry," I said, my stomach gurgling to the contrary.

"Really? Oh. I can't go grocery shopping without getting ravenous. That's why I hate supermarkets. They make everything look so good. It's too hard. Too hard to pass up the Oreos." As if that was why she never went shopping.

"I already ate," I said. "I ate before I went out. I'm not hungry now."

"Oh. All right. If you're not hungry, you're not hungry. We'll have to do dinner together another time. Sometime soon, okay?"

"Sure, whatever. I'm going up to my room."

"Okay, honey. Oh, I almost forgot to tell you. We've picked a date for the funeral. It's going to be next Saturday. Do you want to... to work on something to say? It would be nice if you said something. Or read something. You could read from one of your grandma's old books. She would have liked that, I think."

"Sure, maybe." My feet started to itch. "I'll work on it. Can I go now?"

"You don't feel like watching TV? We could watch something together. Or a movie. We could go rent... something." She had the worst taste in movies and she always, *always* cried at the end.

I wanted to say yes. No, that's not true. I knew that I should say yes, that a good daughter would. That in the TV-movie version of my life, my mom and I would find some stupid way to bond and we'd cling to each other through the hard times—through times like this. I knew that I should have said yes. But I couldn't. Her sad eyes were completely repulsive. They reminded me too much of mine.

"No," I said, "I'm pretty tired."

"Oh. Okay. Sure. We'll talk later. Good night, honey."

"Night, Mom."

I climbed the stairs to my bedroom, lay down on top of my covers, and tried to ignore the empty feeling in my stomach and that it was only six o'clock. Eventually, I slept.

3

I woke up Sunday morning with a headache. The sun coming through my bedroom window—it was still sunny, didn't nature know it was January in Toronto?—pinned me to my bed and I didn't get up until after two. The phone rang as I sat nursing my third bowl of Life cereal, but I let it ring to the machine. I checked the call display: Megan. She didn't leave a message, as usual, but called back two more times in a row. After three unanswered calls, she deigned to leave her name at the beep.

"Hi, this message is for Kat. It's Megan. Let me know when you get this, okay? I need to talk to you before school tomorrow. Call me."

I picked up the portable phone and pressed "talk." The dial tone burned in my ear and I pressed "end." I tied the bathrobe I'd been wearing tighter around my waist, loaded my spoon and cereal bowl into the dishwasher, and took the phone into the living room. I curled up on the couch by the window and turned the phone over in my hands, daring myself to make the call. I pressed "talk" again and, before I could back out of it, dialled the number I'd known by heart since I was six years old.

"Hello?" said the voice on the other end. It was either Megan or her younger sister June; I'd always had trouble telling their voices apart on the phone.

"Hey," I said, "Megan?"

"No, it's June. Hold on, let me get her." Then, with her mouth probably only a few centimetres away from the receiver, she yelled, "Meg-an! Phone!"

A minute later, Megan picked up the line. "Hang up the phone, June," she said, "I've got it." We sat in silence for a few seconds before Megan shouted, "June! The phone, hang it up. This conversation is not for you." We waited for it, then heard June's resigned sigh followed by a click.

"Hey," I said, "how are you?"

"I'm great. Really great, actually. It's been a really amazing break. You'll never guess what finally happened. Oh my god, I still can't believe it. But I feel like I have to tell you, you know? This is, like, historical."

I was waiting for her to ask about my grandmother. I was

sure the word must have travelled between our families by now, but she went on and on about the ski weekend her family had been on and how in love she was with Pat. Pat, who up until a few weeks before had seemed only slightly more interested in her than in his calculus homework. He was just the latest in a string of guys who had all been more interesting, more important, than me. This was someone who I used to call my best friend. When had a dumb crush become bigger than that? Some idiot jock was only going to try to feel her up in the hallway and then brag about it to his brain dead friends. Get her fall-down drunk at a party and then leave her there. The guys she went after were all the same—pretty boy assholes who treated her like crap.

"It's been so cool," she said, "Patty emailed me, like, four times while my family was away skiing. I can't believe how close we are now. I mean, I knew sleeping with him would change the way he felt about me, but I didn't think he'd care so much. He can be really sweet, you know."

"Whoa," I said, "you guys had sex?"

"Yeah, we did. It wasn't a big deal. Okay, maybe it was. Yeah, all right, it was. It was a huge deal. It was historical. It was last Saturday. His parents weren't home so we had, you know, privacy. He was totally romantic about it, too, it was so cute. Like, he lit these candles that smelled like vanilla and played some music. It did kinda hurt, but it wasn't that bad really, not as bad as I thought it was going to be. He was so sweet. After it was all over we watched *The Lion King* together and he made us scrambled eggs with hot dogs."

The Lion King? I remembered racing with her to the movie theatre after school in grade six to go see it. We'd told our parents we were going to a G-rated movie about a bunch of cartoon animals, but when we got there Megan declared that *The Lion King* was for babies, and instead we scared ourselves stupid watching *Leprechaun 2*.

"That's great," I said. "Cool, wow. Good for you. For you guys. That sounds... nice."

"It was great, I felt really good about it. I was totally ready, you know?" She didn't care what I thought at all, she was just telling me the story to brag about it. It was so obvious.

"And, I mean, you guys were, uh, safe, right?"

"Oh yeah, of course."

"Good, that's good." What else did she expect me to say?

"Yeah, good. Anyway, I also just wanted you to know that I'm totally over everything that happened this fall and I just want us to be able to be friends again, okay? It's so important to me. I mean, I know Pat and I are going to be pretty busy this semester since he's agreed to help out with the prom committee—which is so amazing because we really need the

18

male perspective on the event because, hello, the guys are all going to be there too—but I want you to know that I'm totally over it and I want us to still be friends."

"Cool, yeah, that-that's great. I'm glad. That'll be nice."

"You sound weird," she said. Apparently she was listening to me. "I kinda thought you'd be a bit more relieved that I'd forgiven you. Is something going on?"

"Oh yeah, I was going to tell you. I'm surprised my mom didn't tell your mom already." I took a breath in and hoped I wouldn't cry. "But, uh, my grandma died. She died on New Year's."

"Oh my god, no, seriously? I'm sorry. That's so sad. That's so, so sad. That's awful! I'm so sorry. Which one?"

"My mom's. Her mom. My, uh, my mom's mom." I coughed, but apparently I was all cried out.

"God, and she died on New Year's Eve? That's so sad, that's terrible. How old was she?"

"Ninety-two."

"That's pretty old. That's still sad, though. That's so sad." She sounded fake, she sounded so, so fake.

"Yeah, I know."

"Are you, like, okay?" Like she cared.

"Sure, I'm fine." As if I was going to tell her the truth. "I'll be fine. You know, eventually."

"Wow, okay, wow. I don't know what to say."

"It's fine. You don't have to, like, console me. I'll be all right."

"Do you want to talk about it or anything?"

Of course, of course, of course I did. The words were straining against my lips like they were trying to break down a wall. But I knew I couldn't trust her. Even though I somehow still wanted her to be the person I could talk to, I knew she wasn't, not anymore. Not since the fall.

"Not really," I said. "No."

"You're sure? Well, I guess I'll just see you tomorrow then."

"Yeah, sure."

"Okay," she said. There was a big, long, enormous pause. "Bye, Kat."

"Bye. Um, hey, Meg?"

"Yeah?"

"How much good do you think you could do with fifty dollars? I just mean, like, what could you do with money that would be, you know, really good?"

"Huh?" she said. "Well, I mean, the prom committee could definitely use more money. We're going to wind up having to decorate the hall with, like, dollar store crêpe paper, considering the state of our finances. But we'll be doing candygrams soon and I think it'll be a good fundraiser. Why're you asking?"

"Oh, nothing. Never mind, forget about it. I don't know, I'm kind of a mess right now."

"You want me to come over or something?"

Yes. No. No. Yes.

"No, it's fine. I've got to go anyway, my mom and I are, uh, going to bake cookies."

"Okay. See you."

"Bye."

After I hung up with Megan I could feel the dull throbbing behind my eyes getting worse. I went up to my room and turned off all the lights. I closed the blinds and curled up on my bed with my knees up to my chin. I tried to remember every nasty thing Megan had done to me since we were kids—how much I'd let her get away with because she'd always told me I was her best friend and best friends weren't allowed to be mad at each other. We didn't really have much in common, not anymore. For the past three years it seemed like we'd mostly been maintaining our friendship for the sake of nostalgia. I didn't know whether I could trust her when she said she'd forgiven me for what had happened, but it hurt too much for me to spend any more time thinking about it.

Mom came home around eight that night, and when I told her I hadn't eaten dinner, that I'd had a migraine that lasted all day, she insisted we sit down together.

"I'm worried about you," she said as we set the dinner table for our microwaved entrées.

"What about me?"

"Well, it just seems like you're taking your grandma's death pretty hard." She flashed her sympathy smile, the one I'd seen her give so many times when she presented a sob story on air.

"It *is* hard."

"Honey, of course it is, of course. It's hard on all of us. But is there something else that's bothering you? Whatever it is, you can tell me."

Because she'd been such a good listener in my life so far? From a young age I was aware of how disinterested my mom was in me. She always seemed to be waiting for the pause in conversation when we could talk about her. Like in some way I was the parent.

"It's nothing," I said, "it's just Grandma. I'm just sad, okay? I'm really, really sad."

"And that's okay, that's normal. But I don't want to see you cutting yourself off from the rest of the world because you're so sad. It's not healthy."

What did she know about healthy? "Okay," I said. "Fine."

"Yes. Well. I've noticed you haven't had Megan over in quite a while. Is everything all right between you two? I've been there before and, trust me, fights with your girlfriends can get pretty nasty."

"We're not fighting. She's just been busy, that's all. She's dating this new guy, Pat."

"Oh, well, good for her, that must be nice. But you can bring other friends over here too, you know. I'm just worried that maybe you're alone too much, kiddo. It might be nice if you could talk to someone about how you're feeling. Obviously you don't feel like talking to me."

She sounded more relieved than anything, but at least she was trying. Still, nothing about the conversation felt like a genuine attempt. Maybe if we'd been eating off of actual plates.

"I'm fine," I said. "Really, I like it this way. I don't need to talk, I just need time to, you know, figure it all out."

"Sure, okay. Everyone goes through things like this differently. Just don't dig yourself in too deep, okay? If you keep up this anti-social act you're going to alienate a lot of people. A lot of would-be friends. Boyfriends, too."

Because now was clearly a great time to talk about my lack of love life. For someone whose job it was to talk for a living, she was really awful at it.

"Okay," I said. "I'll try harder."

"I just want you to be happy."

I wanted to believe her. It would have been so much easier if I could.

"And I just want to be sad. Right now. I need to."

"All right, fine, I understand. But eventually you'll want to be happy again. And I don't want you to find you've run out of options."

"Sure," I said, "great." I picked up my fork and soggy paper tray, carried them to the kitchen and threw them both away. I climbed the stairs to my bedroom, twisted the dimmer switch on my wall up a little bit so that there was enough light to read by and picked up my copy of *In The Skin of a Lion*. Mr. Grayson had assigned it to our English class before the break, but I kept putting off reading it because every time I sat down with it I couldn't get the words to make sense.

> *This is a story a young girl gathers in a car during*
> *the early hours of the morning.*
> *Girl, car, morning, young,*
> *this in a story is early*
> *the.*
> *a a of the*
> *hours gathers during*

a morning story, early
gathers
young girl, car.
this is during the
a a hours of
the in

    They kept jumping around the page, refusing to stay still and be read. I was waiting for the story to make sense, but it felt like poetry layered over a dream and I couldn't get a feel for the characters at all. It didn't help that squinting at the beautiful, nonsense words made my head hurt even more. I knew we'd be starting to talk about it the next day at school, but I gave up, I couldn't do it. I stuck the scrap of paper I was using as a bookmark back into the novel and set it down by my backpack on the floor. I turned off the light, punched my pillow a few times to fluff it up, lay down and closed my eyes.

My alarm went off at eight o'clock. I yawned with a grimace then rubbed the heels of my hands into my eye sockets. I ran my hands over my face and back down through my hair: greasy, knotted. I thought about how Megan used to insist that we wake up looking our best when we had sleepovers. We spent what seemed like forever washing and braiding each others' hair and doing our makeup before bed, only to wake up to pillows smeared with lipstick, mascara and eyeshadow, like some freaky mask.

I squinted and turned toward the window; a grey day.

I brushed my teeth and went down to the kitchen. The house was already empty. My parents had both left for work. I grabbed a granola bar to eat on my way to school—chocolate chip with tiny spongy marshmallows—and put the box back in the cupboard. I turned to leave and then paused, opened the cupboard again, took a second bar and put it in my backpack. I put on my boots and my enormous down coat, wrapped my scarf around my neck and put on my hat. I reached into the pockets of my coat, but found only one glove. I stomped around looking for the other for a few minutes before I realized that I was late. I shoved my one ungloved hand deep into my pocket and locked the door behind me.

It wasn't a long walk to school, but the puddles from a rainy December had frozen over and I had to be careful where I stepped on the sidewalk. I took side streets for a while, until I got down to Bloor. I stopped walking and reached around into my bag for my Discman. I put my headphones on and hit "play." It was the CD that had been my favourite for months—Everclear, *So Much for the Afterglow*—but that morning it sounded awful. All I could think about was how stupid it was that someone so rich and famous, the band's singer, could still be so hung up on his parents' divorce when he was a kid. And the song that came next, the one about how if he had money he'd buy his girlfriend a house, just seemed like sentimental fluff. That song had played endlessly on the radio for months. It sounded so good the first time I heard it. Maybe money didn't make him and his band any happier, but I had a feeling that they were doing better than they let on in their mope rock anthems. The songs were still poppy and hypnotic, though, and they helped distract me from the frost creeping up my nostrils as I walked.

I made it through the school's front doors and down the hall to my locker. I spun the dial on my combination lock without thinking, relying on the sense memory of the hundreds of times I'd unlocked it before, and the shackle clicked out of the base. I took out the binders and textbooks I'd need for my morning classes and then locked it again. I checked my watch. If I didn't run into anyone in the halls, I'd be just in time for English. Slinging my backpack onto my shoulder, I took the stairs at the far end of the hall up to the second floor.

The halls were full of kids yakking about their Christmas breaks and hugging like they hadn't seen each other in years. I avoided making eye contact with anyone and had almost made it to Mr. Grayson's room when Megan saw me at the other end of the hall and waved me over. She was standing with her arm linked through Pat's, then moved to hold his hand and kept switching her grip as she spoke to me.

"Hi, Kat," she said, "it's so good to see you. I'm so sorry about your grandma. Really."

"Thanks," I said. "It's fine, I'll be okay."

"You're sure you're all right enough to be back here and everything? Like, you feel good enough to go to class?"

"I'd feel a lot worse just sitting around doing nothing," I said, which was actually sort of true. But then Megan started to give me her most vile "poor you" look—her pity was so forced and obligatory it was embarrassing—so I cracked a lame joke. "I must be really sick if I'd rather be here than at home."

"Yeah, totally. Ha!" Her laugh was jagged, forced. "That's funny. You know, if you're looking to keep yourself busy and be, like, involved in something, it's not too late to join the prom committee. It might be a good idea for you to have some kind of extracurricular on your transcripts for university."

Back at the beginning of grade nine, I had told Megan I was thinking of joining yearbook. She told me that only goody-goody losers joined clubs.

"You might even make some friends. Everyone on the committee is really cool," she said.

This from the girl who, when we were kids, used to make me pinky swear that I would never go over to anyone else's house after school.

"Thanks," I said. "I'll think about it."

"Great. Oops, we're going to be late, Patty!" She flashed me one more "poor you" look as Pat winced at his nickname.

"See you guys around," I said, making a break for Grayson's classroom.

He was just closing the door when I got there. "Katherine," he said, "come on in. You're just in time."

Grayson gave us a speech kind of like the one he'd made back in September. He wanted to be clear that it was never too late for any of us to redeem ourselves from the less-than-stellar work ethic we'd exhibited in the fall term. I liked Grayson for that, his even-handedness, but it also made him look like a pushover. I wanted a teacher who I felt I had to work hard for, someone who'd reward me above anyone who didn't care as much as I did. But Grayson always said he didn't believe in picking favourites, so we were all treated equally and I couldn't make myself care about his class.

"So," he began, "*In the Skin of a Lion*. Show of hands, who actually read the book over the holidays?"

A few of us raised our hands.

"Okay now." He smiled a cheesy, teacher grin. "Be honest, how many of you finished the book?"

I put my hand down and so did everyone else.

"All right," he said, "that's okay. How about we start by reading a passage near the beginning to get a feel for Ondaatje's prose. Would anyone like to volunteer to read?"

No hands, no surprise.

"Fair enough, we're all a little stiff, I suppose." One of the guys in the back row with giant, fuzzy raver pants snickered, but Grayson acted like he didn't get the joke. "I'll read first.

Turn to page twenty-five in your books, please."

> *A truck carries fire at five AM through central To-*
> *ronto, along Dundas Street and up Parliament*
> *Street, moving north. Aboard the flatbed three*
> *men stare into passing darkness—their muscles*
> *relaxed in this last half-hour before work—as if*
> *they don't own the legs or the arms jostling against*
> *their bodies and the backboard of the Ford.*

It was kind of sad, sitting there, watching him read like that. Grayson put on this totally different voice as he stood and pronounced the words. He sounded kind of like the people at the open mic poetry nights my mom had taken me to a couple of years ago; they all seemed to speak in the same rhythm. This was during a brief period when she decided I had literary talent and that this talent needed to be nurtured—that and she was off work for a few weeks recovering from a facelift. I almost cried when she asked me to go the first time. We hadn't spent any real time together in months, and even though I was embarrassed to be hanging out somewhere cool—the back room of a trendy bar—with my mom, my joy at being invited was my real shame.

All the poets on those nights were performers and it felt totally weird. You could tell there was a kind of narcissism hiding between and underneath their words, the speaker's love of their own voice that embarrassed the crowd. And right then, in class, it felt exactly the same.

"So," Grayson said when he finally finished, "does anyone have any thoughts about what I just read?" Nothing. "Does anyone know those street names?"

"Duh," someone said. "It's Toronto."

"Yes, exactly. And how does it feel to be reading a book that engages with the world you know?"

"Aren't books always kind of engaged with the world we know?" one of the guys who was also in my gym class asked.

"Not that geeky sci-fi shit you read!" one of his buddies shouted.

"All right, I think we're getting a little off topic here," Grayson said. "Why do you think Ondaatje chose to be so explicit—" another giggle from the raver guy "—with his descriptions of the city? Do you think the novel could have been set somewhere else, or is Toronto's identity central to the story?"

"Well, Mr. G, if you're bringing it up it probably means that Toronto is important to the book. You kind of spoiled your own question," Gym Guy said.

Why did Grayson let stuff like this happen? I wanted him

to put my snarky classmate in his place so badly, but all he did was shrug and push the sleeves of his Cosby sweater up to his elbows.

"Fine, James," Grayson said, "fair enough. But what role do you think the city plays in the story?"

"I didn't read the book."

"Okay, then based on what I read to the class, what do you think Ondaatje is saying about Toronto?"

"Um, I guess he's saying that, like, the city, um... the city works hard?"

"And?"

"And, I don't know, that there's a lot of people that help build it?"

"Okay, good, that's good. We're getting somewhere here. With *In the Skin of a Lion,* Ondaatje is unearthing and romanticizing the contributions made by early citizens of Toronto, many of them immigrants, to the city we know today."

"So it's, what, some secret history?" asked Gym Guy's buddy.

"In a way, yes. Using a stirring, tantalizing, postmodern structure, Ondaatje—"

"Mr. G, what's postmodern?" Gym Guy's buddy again.

"Mr. Grayson, it's time for us to go." Raver Guy this time.

"Do we really have to finish the whole book for next

class?" asked Gym Guy.

The bell rang and I left class quietly, shielded by my needy classmates.

The rest of the morning was fine, or at least as fine as could be expected. I ran on auto-pilot through my current events class, where it always seemed like I was the only one who ever bothered to read the newspaper—even though I hadn't touched one since before Christmas—and then it was lunch. I went to my locker, got my backpack and walked to one of the falafel places close to school.

The little string of bells hanging over the entryway rang dully as I opened the door to the restaurant and plodded, with the weight of my giant backpack, to the lineup at the front counter. I ordered my sandwich with extra tahini and sat down at one of the small tables in the back. The sauce had dribbled onto my plastic tray, my coat and my jeans before I realized that there was a hole at the bottom of the paper wrapper. I licked my napkin and tried to blot out some of the mess, but I knew the stains weren't going to come out. I felt my eyes tearing up and sat there willing myself not to cry in public, hardly believing what a pathetic wreck I'd become. Every tiny thing reminded me of how hopeless I was, how I had no one left to cheer me on and take my side. I couldn't do anything right anymore. I took a small bite out of my sandwich; the falafel patties were cold.

I continued licking and blotting, trying to keep my head down, trying to blink back the tears, and noticed three girls from school enter the shop, talking loudly. One of them was Marie, a girl with big wireframe glasses who was in my chemistry class, but I only vaguely recognized the girls she was with, they might have been a year younger, in grade eleven. Marie kept laughing in this over-the-top, cackling way that was so loud it made my teeth hurt. The girls ordered their sandwiches—two falafels and one chicken shawarma—paid and sat down at the table next to mine. Marie, Shawarma Girl and Girl Number Three. I took my copy of *In the Skin of a Lion* out so they wouldn't think I was eavesdropping and sat studying the pages, unable to focus on any of the words.

"You guys," Marie said, "you should have been at that show on New Year's Day. It was, like, so amazing. It was the best show I've ever been to, I swear. And I didn't even mind coming home smelling like smoke afterwards, because it was just so, so, so incredible. Okay, maybe I did mind the smoke. Can you believe people are allowed to smoke inside like that? They should seriously ban it, it's so disgusting."

Jack used to tell me about how his mom always got upset when he came home from shows—shows he wasn't even supposed to go to because they were 19+, but he had a good fake ID—reeking of stale cigarette smoke. She never quite believed him when he said he didn't smoke. Maybe that's why he started smoking.

Jack. Megan. Megan. Jack.

Marie kept talking; it seemed like she was always talking. "There was this guy with a cigarette, like, right in my face for the whole first band's set. I didn't want to say anything 'cause he was this total neanderthal Nazi dude, but I finally just said, like, 'Excuse me, but could you please take your poison somewhere else? I'm trying to enjoy the music.' Man, I wish there were more straight edge bands in Toronto. Then I wouldn't have to put up with stupid stuff like that every time I want to enjoy some music. It's so lame that there's, like, no scene here. I'm, like, the only person who ever wears Xs to the shows we go to."

Xs? I'd seen Marie come to class with them marked on her hands before. It was pretty weird, but they also made her look kind of tough.

"I don't know," said Girl Number Three, "I listened to that XgloryX tape you sent away for. That stuff was pretty intense. I'm kind of glad we don't have a bunch of bands like that here."

These girls still listened to tapes? I thought everyone in the world had switched to CDs.

"I don't even like those guys anymore," Marie said. "They're so immature, totally hardline, they take a good thing way too far. Like all that stuff they say about killing jocks who drink beer. It's just stupid, it makes us all look bad."

There are a few jocks at school who we could all live without, I thought.

"Something makes you guys look good?" Shawarma Girl asked.

"Come on," said Marie, "even you like Minor Threat. And they, like, invented straight edge!"

"They did?" said Girl Number Three.

"Yeah," said Shawarma Girl, "like twenty years ago. Straight edge doesn't mean anything now. Like, 'don't smoke, don't drink, don't fuck,' whatever."

"'At least I can fucking think,'" said Marie.

It was like they were all speaking French. I knew some of the words they were saying, but I couldn't figure out what it all meant even though I knew it was something I should be able to understand.

"You really are 'out of step with the world,'" Shawarma Girl said.

"Huh?" said Girl Number Three. "Are you guys quoting something?"

"It's a Minor Threat song," said Marie, "called 'Out of Step.'"

"My point," said Shawarma Girl, "is that this stuff is totally ridiculous: the movement's dead."

"No," Marie said, "no way, absolutely not. My edge means something to me. It's who I am. So how can it be dead?"

"Whatever," said Shawarma Girl.

"Anyway," Marie said, "what was I saying? Oh yeah, this guy at the show. So he was, like, so surprised that I actually stood up for myself that all he did was give me a total death glare and then go back to the bar. It was kind of cool, actually, standing up to him. I can't believe you guys both missed it!"

I had to admit that did sound kind of cool. Marie was definitely tough. Weird, but tough. Like nothing phased her. Or, if it did, that she just didn't care.

"I was so wiped all day," said Shawarma Girl, "how did you have any energy after that party?"

"You may recall that I wasn't drinking at said party and that I didn't puke on anyone's shoes either."

"Can you spare us the lecture, Marie, please?" said Girl Number Three. "We had a good time."

"Look," said Marie. "I'm not going to pretend that I had

a better time at the party than you guys, but the show was amazing and you totally missed it because you were too hungover! Anyway, whatever. One of the opening bands was so incredibly cool, just amazing. Awesome. I bought their CD and I got their singer's email! We talked for, like, forever after their set. They sounded so cool, kind of like Jawbreaker meets Rainer Maria. It was, like, the best night ever."

I think Jack told me about Rainer Maria once, but when I looked them up online all I could find was a bunch of stuff about some dead poet.

"Whoa," said Girl Number Three, "that sounds cool. So? Are you gonna email the singer?"

"Definitely, definitely. I thought maybe I'd ask them to let us be their opener the next time they play a show downtown. I'm gonna tell them we're a cool up-and-coming young band, excited to start playing some real shows. Seriously, their sound and their style is pretty much exactly what I want us to be like. They were so cool."

"Yeah, you mentioned that," said Shawarma Girl. "Don't you think we should pick a band name before you start booking us shows? We only have, like, two and a half songs anyway. That's not even half a set."

"So, we'll learn some covers," said Marie. "And we'll practise tonight after school—who's in?"

I wanted in. At that moment, without half a clue what they were talking about and not daring to look up from my book, I wanted in. There was carelessness and maybe even danger, here. There were things to believe in and people to fight for them. It was pure lust, an instant infatuation. I just knew.

"Sorry," said Girl Number Three, "I've got to get home to look after my brother."

"I guess we could practise some time this weekend," said Shawarma Girl.

"Yeah," said Marie, "okay, sure. I'm going to try and write another song by then. This is going to be excellent."

"Sure," said Girl Number Three, looking at her watch. "Shit, we're gonna be late. We better get back to school." They each brought their trays over to the garbage, dumped the paper wrappings of their sandwiches into the bin and stacked their plastic trays on the box above.

I waited a minute or so before doing the same.

After lunch I had history and chemistry. As I walk into Ms. Dixon's fourth period chem class, I saw Megan and Pat sitting next to each other at the back of the room. Anxious to avoid them, I slipped into an empty desk near the front before they noticed me. I heard the stool to my right scrape against the linoleum and looked over as Marie took the seat next to mine.

"Hey," she said, "Katherine, right? I just saw you at Sarah's Falafel. That place is great, isn't it? Totally the best. The best. You mind if I sit here?"

"Yeah," I said, moving my seat away slightly, "sure."

"Sweet. I have to sit up pretty close to the board because my glasses seriously suck. I need to get a new prescription or something. It's all like, 'Whoa, I'm blind!'"

"Oh, huh. I see."

"Ha! I don't!" She pulled her textbook and her binder out of her bag and slapped them down loudly on our desk. "Oops," she said, "sorry."

"No problem."

We sat next to each other for the rest of the period without saying much. I wanted to ask her the name of the band she'd been talking about at lunch, but I didn't want her to know I'd been listening in.

Marie had kind of a good thing going. She was a geek and everything, but she didn't care, or at least she was better at faking it than most of our classmates. It was pretty clear that she had a whole other life outside of school, so I guess it didn't bug her that she was somewhere around the bottom of the social ladder. She had her friends, her straight edge smugness—whatever that was all about—and a rotating collection of band tees that all seemed to make her pretty happy. On the surface, anyway. As much as anyone can be in high school.

Marie always looked like she needed more sleep, but was outspoken about how she didn't believe in taking drugs, even caffeine. She took being straight edge pretty seriously, it seemed, and she got made fun of for it a lot—I remember some girl once yelling, "Who do you think you are, Bif Naked?" at her, but Marie didn't even give her the satisfaction of a response—it just never seemed to phase her. And now, apparently, she and her friends had started a band.

A year ago, I would have totally ignored her if she'd tried to sit next to me in class. Which is a shitty thing to admit, but Marie was, is, just so out there—so loud and so out of step—without even realizing that she's left the Earth's orbit. But right then, that afternoon in chem class, I needed two things: new CDs and someone to talk to who wasn't Megan. It seemed plausible that Marie could help me out. So, as we were packing up our bags to leave for the day, I turned to her and said, "Hey, do you remember which pages Dixon assigned? I kinda spaced out the last ten minutes of class."

"Yeah, for sure." She opened her binder and as she flipped through to find where she'd written out the homework a bunch of different fliers she'd tucked inside fell to the floor. "Oops!" she said. "Do you mind grabbing those for me?"

I bent down to pick them up and looked at each one in turn. "Are these all for shows?" I asked.

"Yeah, there's some cool stuff happening at the Kathedral in the next couple of weeks. You ever been there? It's totally gross—like STD central, ha!—but it's also, like, the only all-ages venue in town that has shows every weekend." Looking at the flier in my hand she asked, "You ever heard of Falter? They're so great. They're playing the Reverb on Saturday."

"Uh, no, I don't know them. What do they sound like?"

"They're so great. They're punk, but sort of emo, too. I mean, like, it's really raw, emotional music, but it's still kind of pretty and a bit sludgy. Ugh, I hate trying to describe music. Do you want to borrow their CD? It's going to be a great show. I was going to go with my friends, but now neither of them can make it. Do you want to come with me?"

Coming off a near week of sad sack solitude, I was stunned by how much Marie talked. I just stood there, nodding, while she reeled off a list of details about the band, who were totally on the verge of getting huge, but still small enough that their shows were like dysfunctional family reunions. She said they usually played at a place called the Big Bop, a giant purple building at Queen and Bathurst with three venues stacked on top of each other. Most of the shows she went to, she said, were on the main floor, the Kathedral, but sometimes they were on the second floor, the Reverb, or on the third, Holy Joe's.

"So, what do you think?" she asked when I still hadn't said anything in response to all her chatter.

"Yeah," I said, "I guess. Do you mind lending me their CD first so I can make sure I'm into the music?"

"Oh yeah, absolutely! I'll bring it for you tomorrow."

"Thanks, I guess I'll see you then." I waved goodbye to Marie and left the classroom. Megan was standing by her locker at the other end of the hallway and I passed her on my way downstairs.

"Hey," she said, "I saw you got stuck with Marie for chemistry. It's probably not too late to switch seats and sit near me and Pat."

"Oh yeah, well I mean she sat down next to me, there wasn't much I could do. She seems all right, though; I don't want to make a big deal out of it."

"Okay, but if she gets all preachy and straight edge on you just tell her you're not buying it. It's so weird that she's so freaked out about drinking and stuff, like, what's the big deal, you know?"

"Yeah, it is kind of weird."

At home, nothing felt right. Up in my room I took off all my clothes—they were too tight, they were too loose—and left them lying all over my bedroom floor. I lay down on my bed, turned from side to side, then sat up cross legged. I stayed like that, staring into space in just my underwear, for what felt like an hour. When I got cold, I put my sweater back on, went down to the kitchen and nuked three pepperoni and bacon Pizza Pops. I ate them, watching TV in my room, then fell asleep trying to decode more Ondaatje.

> *He talks in English to himself.*
> *He, himself, in to English, talks.*
> *English talks to he in himself.*

5

My alarm went off at seven-thirty the next morning, and at first I had no idea where I was. My morning routine ran in slow motion, and I seemed to be watching from outside myself, just above my head, as I brushed my teeth with Kid's Crest, bubblegum flavoured—the stuff I'd used since I was little, the stuff Megan always used to make fun of me for—wiped my face with an Oxy pad—she'd never had zits, she had no idea how lucky she was—and spread Spring Breeze scented Secret—she used Powder Fresh—under my arms. Every insignificant detail of my morning routine was somehow wrapped up in our friendship, like every product on the shelf had her face on the label. I used to think that it was because we knew each other so well, but maybe matching deodorant was all we'd ever really shared.

I put on the new boots my parents had given me for Christmas, the ones I hadn't taken out of their box since the

47

twenty-fifth. I knew it was Mom's way of weaning me off my old boots—she said they made me look like G.I. Joe—but the new ones did look pretty cool: they came up to just above my ankles and had big, chunky heels. She probably had her assistant pick them out. But when I looked in the front hall mirror, I realized the new boots looked stupid with the outfit I had on. Not having enough time to change, I left the house anyway. As it turned out, the boots didn't have any tread and I wound up falling on my ass twice on the walk to school. Fortunately for my sore ass, I had drama first thing and Mr. Neilson, the failed actor of a teacher, wouldn't let us sit down all period.

"Today, as you all should know, is movement day," he said, "and I see that most of you have forgotten that we wear black on movement day. It's a very important part of the exercise, I hope you all understand that. There's no time for you all to change now, we'll have to make do today. However, next Tuesday, next movement day, I will not be letting anyone into my classroom that isn't wearing all black clothing they can really move in. Understood?"

A few of us nodded.

"All right," Neilson continued, "now everyone find a place in the room for yourself. Walk freely, feel for the room's energy, let your body take you where it wants to go." His voice was dreamy and slow, but also forced and over-practised.

There was a collective giggle before we all broke off into cliques around the room. Mr. Neilson stood in the centre of the room where he'd set up a CD player running from the room's one outlet near the door with an orange extension cord.

"Please be mindful of the cord as you move," he said. "It is vital for this exercise that the music come from the very core of the room, but I don't want to have to deal with any sprained ankles, got that? Good. Now, everyone, begin moving your arms through the space of the room, the space above your head and beyond your body. Experience the existence of your body in the empty space, feel yourself filling up the room."

There were more giggles as my classmates threw their arms in the air or stuck them straight out at their sides, trying to hit their friends who were standing nearby.

"I feel as though some of your aren't taking this exercise very seriously," Neilson said. "Now, I know that you're all in your final term, that you've already sent out all of your university applications and you think that nothing else you do with your time in our little community here will affect your busy and exciting lives afterwards. But, I think you'll find that being comfortable with your own body and with the space it occupies will be an invaluable lesson for your time to come, out in the big, bad, real world."

Someone in the hallway stuck their head in and cough-yelled, "Queers!" A few people in the class started laughing in this obnoxious, overcompensating way.

Mr. Neilson kind of lost it after that. He paused his CD player and went into the hall to try to find the homophobe with a cold. Someone found a decent radio station on the boombox and cranked the volume as everyone but me broke off talking in small groups. After ten minutes, when Neilson still hadn't come back to class, the school's secretary, Ms. Beaton, came in and told us to head to the cafeteria and to bring something quiet to work on.

"Is everything okay with Mr. Neilson?" one of the musical theatre wannabes asked.

"Mr. Neilson is under a great deal of personal strain," Ms. Beaton said.

"Who isn't?" asked one of the goth girls. Her eyebrows were shaved off and then painted on or something. They came down towards her eyes in thin slanted lines and made her look like a cartoon character. I had a hard time not staring. Did she draw them on every morning? That must be so much work.

Ignoring Eyebrows, Beaton said, "He will not be returning to school today."

We all grabbed our bags, filed out of the classroom and walked down the hall to the cafeteria. Amidst all the gossiping about what the deal was with Neilson and how pathetic it was that he couldn't even teach a stupid movement class without having a nervous breakdown, nobody noticed that I slipped out of the school's side doors as we passed them on our way to the caf. I hadn't planned on skipping class and assumed that someone would be out looking for me in a few minutes, so I sat down on the steps by the door, took my Discman out of my backpack and put my headphones on. Black Francis' wild, wailing voice rattled in the space between my ears, sounding so, so good.

Just as I'd closed my eyes—the second song on *Surfer Rosa*, "Break My Body," was so raw and beautiful and driving and kind of sad that I just wanted to feel it wash over me—I heard squeaky boots stomping through the packed-down snow on the lawn coming towards me. I opened them again and saw Marie standing over me, grinning. You could see all her teeth when she smiled and her mouth kind of hung open. Her expression was huge, totally alien.

"Must be some great song," she said. "You look like you're

having, like, a religious experience."

"Oh yeah," I said. "The Pixies. You like them?"

"It's Pixies," she said, sitting down next to me on the steps. "Just Pixies, no the."

"Oh, right, I knew that," I said, embarrassed.

"Oh man," she said, "that sounded so harsh. I'm so sorry, my brother talks like that—he's always correcting me about dumb stuff like song titles and band names. Like when I made him a mix tape for Christmas and put 'Baba O'Riley' on as the first track, but I called it 'Teenage Wasteland,' oh man, he made fun of me for, like, years. So anyway, I didn't mean to go off and sound like him. I didn't mean it that way. Forgive me?" She looked down at my feet. "Wow, those are some boots! How can you walk in those things? I'd be all like, 'Whoa, where's the ground?'"

"Yeah, they were a Christmas present, I don't think I'm going to wear them again. And, uh, don't worry about the other thing." Man, this girl could talk.

"Good," she said and sighed in this really exaggerated way. "I thought maybe I'd spooked my date for the show this Saturday. I mean, not date-date, duh. I just meant my buddy for the show. You know?"

"Right, yeah. I still have to see if it's okay for me to go. There-there's sort of this funeral I have to go to that day. I don't know, you know, how late it's going to go."

"Wow, I'm so sorry, I didn't know. Who died? Oh my gosh, I can't believe I just asked you who died. I'm sure you don't want to talk about it. You must be so sad, I'm sure you don't want to tell me who died."

"It's okay, it was my grandmother. My grandma died."

"Wow," she said. "Wow. That's so sad. I'm sorry."

"It's not your fault. I'm just not sure if maybe there's going to be some family stuff I have to do this weekend, so I don't know if I can make the show."

"Wow," she said for the fourth time. "It's no big deal, don't worry about it. But I brought you my copy of Falter's CD, do you still want to borrow it? It's a really great album; it's kind of sad and sweet, so maybe it would actually be good for you to listen to it and, you know, feel sad, but good. I mean, not good-good, but better. You know?" She unzipped her backpack, reached her arm in and groped around for a while before pulling out the CD. "Here," she said, handing it to me, "I think you'll really like it."

"Great," I said, "thanks. I've actually been looking for some new music to listen to. My CDs all suck. Well," I pointed to my Discman, "except this one."

"Do you want me to make you a mix tape?" she asked. "I mean I know they're not really cool anymore or anything, but do you still have a tape deck? I do, I love making mixes. They're, like, a totally holy experience. Heaven, you know? And mix CDs aren't the same at all, they're way too easy. It's like you can hear the work and the time and care and stuff that someone puts into a mix tape, you know? They're amazing, they're the best."

"It's okay, you really don't need to."

"No, no," she said, putting her hand on my knee, "I want to! Do you want me to make you one?"

"Sure," I said, wishing she could just calm down, could just take her hand off me, could just stop using her outdoor voice all the time. Even though, of course, we were outside.

"Wow," she said, "this is so exciting. This is how you really get to know someone. This is going to be great." She pulled back the sleeve of her oversized plaid blazer to check her watch: a Swatch with a large black X on the face. It must have been some kind of straight edge thing. "Oh man, I didn't realize I'd missed all of first period. Good thing it's our last term, right? Ha!"

"Yeah, I'm so glad we're almost done here."

"I know, right?" She just sat there, grinning at me with her massive, manic smile.

And then, before I could think better of it, I asked, "Hey, what would you do if you had fifty bucks? Like, what do you think you could do with it that was, you know, good?"

"I'd probably spend it all on band T-shirts and CDs," Marie said. "I'm pretty bad with money. Like, seriously, I don't know how I'm going to pay for university, you know? My parents are going to help me out for the first couple of years, I think, but then I'm on my own. So I'm definitely staying in Toronto. And no residence for me. I mean, dorm rooms? Come on. There's no way I could live like that. I totally want to get my own apartment. That way I won't have to deal with, like, drunk frat boys hassling me while I'm trying to write a million-page essay, you know?"

"Right, yeah. I get it."

"Look, listen to that Falter CD today, okay? Tell me if you like it and then I'll have an idea of what to put on your mix tape." She pulled her sleeve back down. "I guess I should get inside. See you soon, okay? See ya." She stood up, turned to walk up the stairs and then stopped. "Oh, wait!" She fished a scrap of paper out of her pocket and took a pen out of her bag. "Here, give me your number." I took her pen and wrote it out. "Great," she said. "See ya."

"Bye," I said, finally exhaling as Hurricane Marie swept past me and into the building. I rubbed my bare hands up and down my sleeved arms, trying to warm them up. I breathed hot air into my freezing hands and held them together over my nose like I was praying. I stood up and stomped my dumb, trendy boots on the steps, then got up and went back inside.

When I got home that night, I went up to my room and put Marie's Falter album into my CD player. I closed my eyes and lay down on my bed. It started with a bass line—thick, thudding, a train slowly picking up speed, helpless to slow the rhythm. There were breaks—stops and starts—when the train finally ran off its tracks. It was aggressive, a mammoth sound, but the choruses were still bright somehow, almost poppy. Jangly guitars coloured with disappointment. The singer's words betrayed the ragged warmth of the sound: on the surface everything was fine, clear and even, but underneath it all the world was falling apart. It reminded me of my Pixies album, but this was new. The singer's wounds were fresh.

I shut off every part of me but my ears, trying to let the pure sound take me over. The hairs on my arms stood on end. That kind of radical honesty, the ability to completely be yourself through your art, was something I knew I'd never be capable of. I cried until the album was over.

I pressed "play" again. And again. And again. I studied the

faces on the back of the jewel case, memorized their names. I read and reread the lyrics in the liner notes.

After my fourth play I felt empty and clean. I picked up some of the dirty dishes I'd left sitting around my room and carried them downstairs to the kitchen where Mom was rummaging through the nearly empty fridge looking for a late dinner.

"Oh, hi honey," she said. "I thought you were asleep already. I would have come upstairs to say hi."

"Nope," I said, "just listening to some music." I opened the dishwasher door and started putting my plates and forks inside.

"That's nice. Hmm, there's not much in here, is there?" she said, closing the fridge door again. "You feel like pizza?"

"I thought you weren't eating cheese anymore."

"I really shouldn't. You should see this new girl they've got doing weather. She looks like she hasn't touched a carb since she was sixteen. Oh well, I'm already the old broad." She paused, waiting for me to protest. I knew I was supposed to—we played this game often enough— but I wasn't in the mood. "Anyway, let's have pizza, just this once. We haven't had any in ages, have we?"

"Not since you took Pizza Pronto off the speed dial."

"Come on, help me find the brochure."

We each searched through the cupboards and drawers of the kitchen until she let out a triumphant sort of hiccup. "Here it is!" she said. "Prontissimo!"

"Great." I just knew I'd wind up having to listen to her whine about the calories she was packing on as soon as she bit into her first greasy piece.

Mom dialled and ordered the pizza: an extra-large with mushrooms and green olives. We sat down on high stools around the kitchen counter and she poured herself a glass of red wine. I had a feeling it wasn't her first of the evening.

"Do you want one, hon?" she asked. "Just this once, it's okay. I think I have some chardonnay, too, in the fridge. You might like that better."

"Red's fine," I said, and poured myself a glass. I took a sip and winced, then took another. "So, what time is the funeral on Saturday?"

"The service starts at one and then there'll be some time for everyone to visit with each other afterwards. I think it's going to be a nice service. Do you have any other plans for the weekend?"

"There was this concert I was thinking of going to, but it's on Saturday, too, so I don't think I'm going to go."

"Why not?"

"I don't know, out of respect? It seems wrong to go out

the same day we bury Grandma."

"Well, we won't be dedicating her ashes until the spring. The ground's too hard right now. It'll be more of a time to remember and for people to pay their respects. More of a wake, really."

"And you don't think it's weird to go from a wake to a divey punk club?"

"I don't want you to go somewhere unsafe, but I think it would be good for you to go out. Is this something you and Megan are going to?"

"No, there's this girl in my chemistry class, Marie. She invited me."

"I think it sounds terrific. I'll give you my cab card so you don't have to worry about taking the streetcar late at night. Where's the concert going be?"

"Uh, it's at Bathurst and Queen."

"Yes," she said, "take a cab. Absolutely. You and Marie both."

"Okay," I said, "whatever." We sat in silence for a few minutes. "Mom? How much good do you think you could do with fifty bucks?"

"Is this about your inheritance? It'll take some time to sort out your grandmother's estate, but I'm sure you'll have a generous amount coming to you. You can spend it however you like, though. Why, were you thinking of donating it to charity?"

"No, No," I said, "that's not what I mean. I don't care about my inheritance. But how much good do you think it would do to donate fifty dollars to charity?"

"Honestly, sweetie? A lot of charities get wrapped up in their administrative fees. For fifty dollars you might help pay for one of their employee's salaries for a few hours. It doesn't mean we shouldn't give money away, we absolutely have to, but I don't think there's much you can do with only fifty dollars."

"Right, I understand."

Dad didn't come home at all that night. Mom said he might wind up sleeping at a hotel near his office if the negotiations went on too late. We live in the Annex, not far from the Financial District, especially in a cab. I felt a tiny vibration—a buzz, I guess, from the wine—and wanted to ask Mom why Dad didn't just come home. Did she think he was avoiding us? Did our grief somehow embarrass him? Was he cheating?

My dad and I were such strangers, I felt like I had no way of knowing what he was really up to. I knew so little about his job—maybe he really did need to stay away all night— and just as little about his marriage, nothing but old stories about him and my mom that seemed so long ago they might as well be about other people.

There were so many questions. Too many. So I bit my tongue, turned a dark blue from the wine.

We finished our glasses of wine and the pizza came. She blabbed on and on about work and I nodded sympathetically, trying to hide the fact that my limbs felt too heavy around me and that my head felt like a cantaloupe balanced on a Q-Tip. I was definitely drunk.

We ate our slices and she had another glass of wine. I went up to bed when it was clear she was aiming to finish the bottle. We all had our coping strategies.

6

The rest of the week, thank God or Whoever, went by quickly. Megan invited me to a party she and Pat were going to Friday night, but I told her I had a lot of stuff to get ready for the funeral. She gave me the kind of look my mom gives homeless people when she has change, but doesn't want to give it to them, but wants them to know she understands what they're going through, even though she doesn't.

After school, in my room, I put on one of Grandma's old necklaces and played Marie's Falter CD again. I turned the TV to some nature show on CBC and muted the sound. I painted my fingernails with a deep purple polish I'd had forever and then accidentally smudged them when they were setting. I used to be good at this. I had a sense of timing, knew when to wait on still-tacky polish and never went outside the lines. It's like somewhere along the way my brain stopped talking to my body, to my hands.

I spent twenty minutes scrubbing my hands with nail polish remover, but in the end they just looked bruised all over. By then my room was stinking with the smell of ammonia and I was feeling pretty light-headed. The phone rang and since no one else was home I picked it up.

"Hi," the voice said, "is Katherine home?"

"Yeah, that's me."

"Oh, hey! That's funny, your voice doesn't sound like you on the phone. I mean, of course it's you, but you sound, you know, different. Anyway, it's Marie, hi! I just wanted to check and see if you thought you might want to come to the show tomorrow, or maybe you're still not sure about all that family stuff you were talking about. I haven't really seen you the last couple of days, other than chem class, and I just wanted to see if you thought you could go or not, or if you wanted to at all."

"Yeah, I think it'll be fine. The funeral's going to be over pretty early it sounds like, so, yeah, it'll be fine. I told you I really liked their CD, right?"

"You said you liked it okay," said Marie, "and I wasn't sure if you were just being polite or whatever, because I know sometimes people get bugged that I can be kind of pushy with music and I didn't want to pester you to see how much you really liked it. But it's amazing, isn't it? It's, like, incredible."

"I liked it a lot. I mean, a lot-a lot. I've listened to it, like, ten times since you lent it to me."

"Wow," she said, "wow. I can't wait for you to see them tomorrow night. They live in Toronto, so they play here all the time. I can't wait for you to see them."

"Right. So I've got my grandma's funeral or wake or whatever in the afternoon, but after I have dinner with my family I should be free to go. What time do you think we should meet at?"

"Well, if we get there early we can hang out and talk to the bands while they set up and stuff. And I really want to talk to Josie, she's Falter's singer. She's so cool."

"Yeah, I know. I love her voice. She's great."

"Oh wow, isn't she? She's, like, my idol or something. She just has it, you know? Oh man. Anyway, the doors open at eight so let's get there for eight-fifteen, okay?"

"Sure, sounds good."

"Great, this is so great. I'll see ya then!"

"Okay," I said, "bye."

A lot of people showed up at the funeral, or the wake, or whatever we were calling it. There were a few speeches, and everyone stood around eating baby quiches, but trying to act like they weren't very hungry. I talked a bit with the family and friends of my grandma who were there, just small talk. And when everyone asked me where I thought I was going to end up for university—they all asked me, it was like every conversation was scripted in advance—I told them I'd applied to a few places: Guelph, Dalhousie, Western and a couple of schools in Toronto. I really didn't know which I would choose, I said, I had to be accepted to one first.

It all felt like an empty gesture. Grandma wasn't there and she wouldn't have cared about a bunch of people moping around a hall, eating cheese cubes and talking about nothing. I had smuggled one of Grandma's books in my purse and I snuck out to the bathrooms and locked myself in a stall with my feet pushed against the door, reading for nearly an hour before someone realized I was missing.

After our extended family had left and it was just us and the caterers my mom had hired cleaning up the hall we'd rented, my parents wanted to take me out for dinner. I protested that we'd been eating all afternoon.

"Come on, kiddo," my dad said. "We haven't all been together since New Year's, just let us spend some time with you." Was it my fault he didn't come home anymore? I hated when he put on the "normal dad" act. It was almost worse than him never being around.

We went to Le Papillon, a French restaurant nearby, and had enough food and uncomfortable conversation to last us at least another month. My dad did that annoying thing where he finds out what my mom and I want to eat and then orders for all three of us. My mom used to say, when I was little and protested being spoken for, that she thought that this habit of his was elegant. From the barely perceptible frown she put on when he ran through the hollow routine this time—those mean little lines around her mouth that are more pronounced each day—it was pretty clear that she doesn't find it so charming anymore. But she still let him do it.

"So, how are things at school?" Dad asked me over dessert—crème brûlées for us and a decaf latte with skim milk for Mom.

"Fine," I said, "it's not like it makes any difference now. My marks are already in for the schools I applied to. I'm just waiting for June."

"That doesn't sound very ambitious," he said. "I thought you wanted to go to law school. You've got to keep your standards up all the way through if you're going to make it."

"When did I say I wanted to go to law school?"

"Come on, you remember. It was about a year ago, and

67

you and I were talking about schools, and you said you thought law would be a good fit. You were excited about it, remember?"

"I remember you telling me you thought I'd be a good lawyer."

"And you would be."

"And I told you there was no way I'd ever do that."

"That's not what you told me."

"Yeah, that's what I said. You never listen to me."

"Alright, easy there." He swallowed a giant lump of custard. "So, what do you want to do?"

"I don't know, I've still got a lot to think about. I don't even know what I want to major in next year." English? Philosophy? Art History? Radical Honesty?

"I'm sure you'll do well, whatever you decide," Mom said. "But you really might want to keep a closer eye on your school work this term. I'd hate to see your marks drop just because you think you've already made it."

"Yeah, I know. I'll try harder."

"Just find a way to love what you're doing," said Mom, "and then it won't seem like work. What about English? You said you liked your teacher, didn't you? What was his name, Grayson?"

"Yeah, he's fine. We're doing *In the Skin of a Lion* now."

"Oh," Mom said, "how nice to be reading a local author. Did I ever tell you that I interviewed Michael Ondaatje? It was right after *The English Patient* came out."

"I remember you wouldn't stop bragging about it when the movie won Best Picture." I said. It should have been a joke, but my voice sounded mean.

"Well," she said, obviously hurt, "I just thought it was sort of neat, that's all."

I knew how TV-movie me would have reacted to this. She would have gotten up out of her chair and wrapped her arms around her insecure but beautiful mother. She'd tell her mom that she was sorry, that she hadn't meant what she'd said, that she knew how important her mother's career was. I could see how it would all play out. Beautiful, perfect. But I felt nothing.

By the time we got home Marie had left three messages on our answering machine.

"Your new friend sounds very eager," Mom said, after the third message had played through.

"She sounds a little nutty," Dad said. "You sure she's all right?"

"She's totally straight edge, if that's what you mean," I said. "She just gets kind of hyper when she's excited. And I can always just get a cab and come home if it gets too weird. Besides, I thought you wanted me to spend time with other people."

"Yes, honey, of course we do." Mom sounded exhausted, like the mask she'd been wearing all day was slowly sliding off, but she didn't have the energy to put it back on.

I went up to my room to change out of the too-tight dress pants I'd been wearing all day and to call Marie. She picked up after one ring, and I could almost see the manic glint in her eyes, having pounced at the receiver.

"Hello?" she said, "Kathy?"

"Hey, yeah, it's Katherine."

"Oh man, I'm so glad you called me back. Sorry for leaving, like, a million messages on your machine. I just wasn't sure how long your dinner was going to be and you know how some people just never seem to check their messages? And I wanted to make sure that mine was the first one on the list and, anyway, how are you?"

"I'm okay. It was kind of a sad day—sort of weird, you know?"

"Yeah," she said, "totally. I understand. My grandpa died last winter, I know how awful I felt afterwards. It was like I was never going to stop being sad. Are you sure you still want to go to the show? It's okay if you don't, it's totally okay, I'd understand."

"No, I want to go. I really need to get out of the house."

"Okay, excellent, that is so good to hear. Where do you want to meet? I was going to take the streetcar down from Bathurst station, do you want to meet me there?"

"Sure," I said, knowing my parents were hoping I'd take a cab. "Meet you there in half an hour?"

"That sounds perfect. So, so, so perfect. I'll see you then!"

"Great. Oh, and Marie? What's the crowd going to be like? I mean... what should I wear?"

"You should never dress for the crowd," she said. "But it'll be pretty casual, probably. You know, sweaters and Converse, that sort of thing. I mean, you don't have to X up like I do or anything. I'm pretty much the only one that does for shows that aren't super punk. I just like to show who I am, even if it means getting ragged on by drunk jerks."

"All right, I've got it. Thanks. I'll see you soon."

Taking a cue from Marie's thrift store style, I got an old sweater my grandmother had knit when I was a kid out of my closet. It was pink and red with a horse rearing up on its hind legs on the front. It was too small, with sleeves that reached just past my elbows, but as I pulled it over my head, it felt right. I put on a pair of baggy jeans and my old boots—the faux army ones—my stupid, puffy winter coat and a bright red wool hat with a pom-pom on it because I knew the walk to the station was going to be freezing. I left the house, waving to my parents who were sitting in the living room trying hard to look interested in each other.

"Call a cab!" Mom said.

"Sure," I said, "I will."

Marie was already on the streetcar platform when I showed up at the station. We got on the next streetcar that arrived, while she talked non-stop about how she liked my hat, how she couldn't wait to see Falter and how their singer Josie was the coolest girl she'd ever seen up close. We got off at Queen Street and Marie took my hand, practically dragging me across the intersection to the giant purple building that stood on the southeast corner.

I'd seen it before, of course, mostly out of car windows while speeding along Queen. The building was pretty hard to miss, but I had no idea that this was the venue Marie had been talking about. Now that we were finally here I felt somehow both attracted and repulsed by the whole thing.

Like I was a magnet with the wrong charge.

"This," Marie said, like a perfect museum tour guide, "is the Big Bop."

"Oh," I said, "yeah."

"Come on, let me show you what's inside."

We walked past a set of doors that were marked *KATH-EDRAL* to a smaller one that said *REVERB*. Above the door was a smaller sign: *HOLY JOE'S*.

"This is it," said Marie, opening the door for me and gesturing for me to walk up the stairs behind it. "After you."

We climbed the stairs, Marie's enormous boots ka-thunking heavily on each step, and arrived at a landing with double doors and a small table pulled out in front of them. Two girls sat behind the table with a cash box and a black Sharpie. The sign they'd taped in front of them said:

> Falter, TEAM, Daydream Nationalists
> $5 / Pay What You Can
> NO PUKING! :-O

While I wondered if that last line was really a threat or just some kind of joke, Marie handed over her five dollars and one of the girls, the one with tiny blonde dreadlocks, drew a star on her hand—Marie hadn't X-ed up, so there was actually space for once. I got out my wallet and gave the girl with an eyebrow ring a twenty. The fifty was still there, sitting guilty. I thought I saw the little guy on the bill—who, William Lyon Mackenzie King?—staring at me. I couldn't believe I'd forgotten about the money. It looked like it was glowing, pulsing in the fold of my wallet, taunting me.

"Seriously?" Eyebrow Ring said. "You guys are, like, the first ones here. I can't break a twenty yet."

"Don't sweat it," Marie said, handing the girl another five. Dreadlocks drew a pukey face like the one on the sign on my hand, and I put the twenty back into my wallet next to the awful fifty. "Lesson one," Marie said, "never bring big bills to a show. At least not before they have a chance to build up some float."

"Oh," I said, "right. Thanks. I guess I kind of owe you one."

"Come on!" said Marie, not caring what she was owed, "let's go find Falter and introduce ourselves."

The club was dirty—the tiles on the floor were scuffed and torn up in places—and it was dark. There didn't seem to be any backstage area for the bands, just the stage itself, an open floor and a little area that was raised up a few steps where the bands had set up merch tables. The stage, and the space in front of it, felt huge around us. The sound booth in the middle of the floor seemed to be the only thing taking up space. We were two of the few people there who didn't have a job to do, and it was hard to believe that the space was going to fill up with people who loved Falter as much as Marie did and as much as I was starting to.

I was feeling self-conscious about nerding out in front of the band I wanted to see so badly, but Marie was pulling her naive confidence card and she took my hand again, walking us around the room and scanning the faces of the few people who had arrived before us. When she found the members of Falter hanging out beside the stage, setting down the amps, guitars and drums that they had just finished hauling up the stairs, she was obviously in her element.

"Hi," she said, walking up to Josie and sticking out her hand, "I'm Marie and this is my friend Kathy. We're big fans."

Marie was totally right. Josie was probably the most beautiful person I'd ever seen close up. She was over six feet tall and wearing massive black boots with buckles up the sides. Her hair was cut short, buzzed on one side and sticking way out on the other. She had rings through each of her nostrils and a streak of purple running through her hair that looked almost natural. She looked at us both, smiled, and without missing a beat said, "Hey, I'm Josie. Good to meet you both."

"I haven't seen you guys play in a while," Marie said. "You used to play here like every month. What happened?" I couldn't believe she was acting this cool about meeting someone so, well, cool.

"Yeah," Josie said, "we kind of felt like we were overplaying Toronto, you know? Plus we've been rehearsing to record our new album. It's going to be a full-length this time, I'm so excited."

"Right on," said Marie. "That's excellent. The EP's so great." Then she turned to me, "Kathy, you should totally buy it." And back to Josie, "This is Kathy's first time seeing you guys."

"I've heard the CD," I said. "I mean, the EP. I really like it. I mean, I think you guys are great. I'm really looking forward to, you know, seeing you play."

"Sweet," said Josie. "I'm so glad to be playing an all-ages show. This is, like, all I ever want to do. Anyway, we've got to tune up and stuff. But I'll see you guys soon."

I stood there with my mouth half hanging open and a weird smile on my face before Marie turned to me and said, "Come on, Kath, let's go get some air before the first band goes on."

"Just a sec," I said, "I need to use the bathroom first." We walked away from the stage, and Marie pointed me towards the girls' room next to the bar. I could see more stairs at the end of where the space narrowed and formed a hallway. "Where do those go?" I asked.

"Holy Joe's," Marie said. "Right on top of it all. It's tiny up there, kind of like being in someone's rec room. It's mostly just for acoustic shows."

"Okay," I said, "cool." And then, once we were inside the washroom, which presumably had some kind of sound-proofing, I shrieked, "That was so amazing! I mean, she talked to us. She was nice, she was so, so cool." I shook my head in disbelief, then did the best I could to use one of the nasty toilet stalls with a door that didn't seem to want to stay closed. "Do you mind holding this shut for me?" I asked.

"Totally," said Marie, "And, yeah! Isn't Josie the best? Plus she's, like, the most beautiful woman in the world."

"Yeah, super pretty." I reached my leg up and flushed the toilet with my boot. "Okay, thanks, you can let go now."

As I washed my hands and Marie looked on, a girl with tonnes of eyeliner, dyed black hair in a bob and a homemade T-shirt that said *SLUT*—was she serious?—came out of one of the stalls behind us.

"I thought that was you, Marie!" the girl said. "It's so good to see you, how's it going?"

"Great," she said, "so great. This is my friend Kathy, Kathy this is Chantal."

"Hey," I said, drying my hands on a paper towel.

"We were just going to go outside for a bit before the first band starts," Marie said. "You want to come with us?"

"For sure," she said, "just let me grab my friend Ivan."

Chantal found Ivan hanging around outside the guys' washroom, eyeing the bar with a thirsty look. Chantal didn't introduce Marie and me, but her friend nodded and said, "Hey," and Marie said, "Hey, Ivan, right? I'm Marie and this is my friend Kathy." I smiled.

Chantal suggested we walk down Queen to a parking lot nearby where we could squat on the concrete parking barriers; there was nowhere else around to sit. The wind was icy and I stuck my hands deep into my pockets to try to keep some of the chill out.

"So, how do you guys know each other?" Marie asked, pointing to Ivan and Chantal, when we'd all sat down.

"Camp," said Chantal. "We sort of dated last summer. He's the best ex I've ever had."

"Yeah," he said, "sure."

"Kath and I go to school together," Marie said, and then, turning to me, "and Chantal and I just know each other from going to all of the same shows."

"Cool," I said. "I really can't wait to see Falter."

"Totally," Chantal said, "but I hear they're going to, like, sign to a major soon and then all their songs are going to be super poppy and boring."

"We talked to Josie," Marie said, "it sounds like she's really excited about their new stuff. Maybe they'll play some of it tonight, then we'll get to see for ourselves."

Ivan reached into the pocket of his coat and pulled out a bottle of orange Gatorade.

"You guys want some?" he asked.

"What's in it?" asked Marie.

"Just Gatorade and some stuff my dad's never going to miss. Vodka, mostly."

"No thanks," she said, "I'm straight edge."

"Yeah," Chantal said, "Pass. I'd rather try to scam a beer than drink any of that stuff you and your friends call... what is it?"

"Jungle juice," said Ivan, taking a slug from the bottle. "You want some?" he asked, pointing the bottle at me.

"Yeah," I said, "sure." I sipped at it and the salty sweetness of the drink didn't cover up whatever it was Ivan had mixed in. I coughed hard.

"It's getting kind of cold," Marie said, ducking her chin

into the folds of her scarf. "I'm going back, the first band'll be starting soon." I knew she was talking to the group, but she was looking right at me when she said it.

"I'll come with you," Chantal said. "I feel like I'm getting kind of old for this."

"Yeah right," Ivan called after her, "'Cause you just turned eighteen."

Chantal turned and gave him the finger and then put her arm around Marie and walked back towards Bathurst. Ivan and I passed the bottle back and forth, not saying much.

"You like the band?" I finally asked when we were almost finished the juice.

"Which one?"

"Falter." Were there other bands?

"Yeah," he said, "they're okay."

Another few minutes of silence.

"Is it weird hanging out with your ex?" I asked.

"We never really dated. We made out once behind the arts and crafts hut. Chantal just likes being dramatic. She's not so bad." He offered me the last sip and I took it. I hadn't been able to eat much at dinner, or any of the baby quiches that had preceded it, and the lightheadedness of the buzz—so different from the wine with Mom—swooped in on me quick. I looked at his eyes and tried to focus on his pupils.

"You have nice eyelashes," I said, trying to centre myself on something, giving my total attention to the tiny hairs that rimmed his eyelids.

And then he moved in to kiss me.

We made out for a while, even though my ass was cold on the concrete and I was sure we were missing the opening band. His breath was the same salty sweet of the drink and his face was the warm centre of the frigid air. He reached for the zipper of my coat and pulled it down, just a bit. He stuck his hand inside. I wanted it to feel right, but it didn't. He was an intruder. His hand was wrong and it was all I could think about.

"You're so warm," he said.

"Stop it."

"Come on, Chantal won't mind."

"No, let's stop. I want to go see the bands."

"You sure you don't want to go somewhere else?"

"No. I'm going back. Do what you want, I'm freezing."

"Fine," he said. "Bitch." He got up and starting walking toward Spadina. "Tell Chantal I left."

"Fuck you!" I wanted to yell—to get the attention of every bored soul on Queen Street and start a riot—but I didn't. In my head I was screaming, but on the street I was silent. Standing up, I felt the full impact of my buzz. I took a step sideways and nearly tripped over the parking lot's jagged asphalt. I steadied myself and watched Ivan walk away. He didn't turn around.

With my hands back in my pockets, I walked back towards the club. I climbed the stairs again, feeling the world slowly shifting sideways, and showed the girl at the door the Sharpie squiggle on my hand. I found Marie and Chantal standing at the front of the stage with a substantially larger crowd around them, including a couple of people who were smoking. The guys in the band in front of us were all hunched over their instruments, looking possessed. The music was an angular assault and it was way too much for me.

"Hey," Chantal yelled over the music, "where's Ivan?"

"He left."

"What, why?"

I was so ashamed, I could feel the rosy burn in my cheeks. It was normal to do those things, to drink and grope; standard teenage stuff. Sure, it was embarrassing to do all that in public, but that wasn't it, that wasn't why I felt so awful and humiliated. It felt wrong. His hand on me. It just felt wrong. And instead of calling the jerk out on it, I'd let him walk away, let him treat me like trash. But Ivan was their friend and I couldn't narc on him without having to tell Marie and Chantal how wrong his hand felt. They'd think there was something wrong with me. And wasn't it my fault anyway for staying out there with him in the first place? Didn't I know what was going on?

"I don't know," I said. "Maybe he was sick."

"I'm not surprised," Marie said, fanning the air around her as someone blew smoke in her direction, "with that shit he was drinking."

The band finished their last song and Marie, Chantal and I sat down around a small table at the back of the room. For once, Marie was actually being quiet. I felt nervous and slow, anxious, like I had to keep the conversation going or I'd give myself away, all of my shame. I just wanted to be normal.

"That was, uh, pretty intense," I said. "Who were those guys?"

"You would've known it if you'd just come inside with us," Marie said. Snapped, actually. She was talking to me like I was dumb, like I was drunk.

"They're called Daydream Nationalists," Chantal said.

"Oh," I said. "I can't wait for Falter, are they on next?"

"No," Marie said, "they're the headliner. There's still another band on before them."

"Who's that?" I asked.

"I forget their name," Marie said. "But I've heard they're not very good. And they don't even have any girls in the band."

"Why do you only like girl bands?" I asked. "I think you can still play and be a band and it doesn't matter who's playing the instruments really, you know, as long as you, like, feel it when they play."

"You're totally drunk," said Marie, looking all pissy and accusatory. "Besides, Jawbreaker are like my favourite band and they're all guys."

"Exception to the rule," I said, "and I am not drunk, I'm not, only maybe a little bit. We didn't drink that much."

"You and Ivan?" she asked.

"Well, yeah. I mean, he offered."

"I guess I just thought we were together in this or something. I mean, I never see you at parties. I thought you didn't drink."

"No," I said, "I don't any—I used to go to parties. I went to parties with Megan. But her parties were always awful, and anyway, we don't talk anymore because I kind of dated her older brother but didn't tell her. So it's not that I don't drink, I just hate everyone, that's all. No offence, Chantal." I was talking, and talking, and talking, and why couldn't I stop my stupid mouth from moving? Why was I telling them all of this?

"Yeah whatever," she said, "none taken. I'm going to go to the bathroom."

"This is stupid," Marie said. "I'm like the only person who doesn't just want to get drunk or stoned or whatever. I'm the only one who cares about the music."

Chantal came back to the table with a bottle of beer in her hand. "I'm so glad my sister gave me her old driver's license when she got her G2. Thank you, Ontario Ministry of Transportation," she said, raising her bottle in salute. "Your graduated licensing system has made this beer possible." She chugged.

Marie spent the whole second band's set sulking and only grudgingly got excited as Falter set their gear up on stage. Josie looked amazing, all glitter and power.

"That's so cool that she doesn't even need someone to help her with her guitar and everything," I said. "She's so cool."

"Why would she need someone to help her?" Marie snapped.

"You're totally right," Chantal said, taking my side. "I mean, I know women can play and all, but when they know their gear, too, it's so great."

"I think all musicians should know how to handle their instruments," Marie said, then she got up from our table to stand right in front of where Josie was now setting up her mic stand. Josie waved from the stage and we could see Marie chatting her up from where we sat.

"God, Marie has such a crush on her, it's so obvious," said Chantal.

"What are you talking about?" I asked.

"She's, like, throwing herself at her and Josie's, like, totally out of her league."

"What? Marie's—she's gay?"

"She says she's bi, but I don't buy it. Ha! Buy it! I didn't even mean it like that. Yeah, she made out with a girl at a show last year and now she's like exploring this, you know, strange new part of herself, which has, like, been there all along. It's totally cool, only she always goes after the ones she can't get. It's, like, torture, watching her."

I looked at the way Marie held her hands and the way she reached out to touch Josie's boots and how she looked up to talk to her. "You're right," I said, half in awe, "she's shameless." We watched them for a few more minutes before Josie and her band walked off stage for a minute, then came back on, took their places and told everyone to come up front. By then the place was pretty full, and Chantal and I rushed to the front to find a spot where we could see.

The band was incredible. They played the whole CD—the

EP—all the way through, then Josie said, "Okay guys, we're going to play some new songs for you. We've been working really hard, so we hope you'll like them." And just as they were about to start into the first one, she held up her hand and said, "Wait! One more thing. I wanted to say thanks to the two girls who hung out before the show. It means a lot to be able to play a show in a venue where everyone's welcome, and we want to see more bands up here with us, more girls making music and more all-ages shows. Okay, let's go!" I could see Marie's whole body light up, and my own face broke into a wild grin.

And the new stuff was maybe even better than the CD. Josie had this unearthly yowl and she'd tear herself apart right in front of us, then she'd get all quiet and sweet and innocent-sounding before letting it rip again, and I was stuck in my place thinking about how amazing it all was and how I wanted to stop thinking about how amazing it was and just be in the moment, but I didn't want to close my eyes because then everyone would think I was a total weirdo. Then, Josie caught my eye and smiled as she started into the song's final chorus and I totally fell apart. My head was spinning, so I grabbed Chantal's sleeve and said, "Hey, I've got to go. Tell Marie I said bye."

"Okay," Chantal said, "get home safe."

I flagged a cab coming up Bathurst and rode it up to

Bloor and through a few Annex side streets to my house. We pulled up outside, I paid the driver with Mom's cab card, and stumbled out of the car and into the house.

My head was still spinning when I got into bed, with Josie's smile and Ivan's breath and Marie's scowl all running on a loop through my brain. My clothes smelled like a carton of cigarettes, I realized as I lay down, but I was too exhausted to change them and I fell asleep in my jeans.

7

The next day, Sunday, I tried to move as little as possible. I read more Alice Munro and took a bath until my fingers were all puckered and the water had turned cool around me. I waited for Marie to call, but she didn't. I thought about writing her a letter about what had happened, telling her how I wasn't sorry for drinking but that I thought Chantal's friend was a real asshole. A couple of times throughout the day I sat down with a pen and piece of lined paper, but I couldn't make myself write the words.

I thought about her while I was in the tub, kept picturing her hands. I thought about Josie and Ivan, too. The same endless loop that had played through my head while I tried to find sleep the night before kept rolling on, and I slid under the faucet as the bathtub filled with water. I fiddled with the knobs to make the water pressure stronger, then arched my back to get the angle just right. Josie and Ivan and Marie.

Josie and Ivan and Marie. Josie and Ivan and Marie, and the warm water where it fell and made me feel so good. I felt the ripples rise through me and into my belly. Josie and Ivan and Marie and the water. Josie and Ivan and Marie. And I came. Then I sat there, in my pool of shame—for the act, for my thoughts, for everything—for most of the afternoon.

I sat down to do my week's worth of homework, stopping only to eat some leftover pizza with the end of a bottle of wine I'd snuck up to my room from the rack that was always overflowing. Mom and Dad were both out—together, I hoped—so neither one noticed when I brought the empty bottle down a few hours later and placed it next to the other empties in the recycling.

I'd finally made some headway with *In the Skin of a Lion*, and probably the wine helped me wrap my mind around Ondaatje's words. We were only going to be spending one more week on the book, so I should have been on to the next one already. But it was driving me crazy that I couldn't get into a book that was supposed to be so beautiful and was supposed to be a story about Toronto—the tiny part of the world that I knew. Besides, we were reading *Catcher in the Rye* next and I'd basically memorized that book when I was fourteen.

So, I was reading about some labourers tunnelling under

Lake Ontario, stopping only long enough to take a photograph for publicity's sake, all these people struggling to make a new waterway for the city. The main character, Patrick, is digging below the lake and he feels the whole continent in front of him. It made me feel claustrophobic and totally insignificant. I closed the book and tried to sleep.

In a dream, I was digging a hole in the back yard, but it kept filling itself back up with dirt every time I put down my shovel.

The next day at school was uneventful. Marie avoided me and clung to her friends, Shawarma and Number Three, and I tried to act like it didn't bother me. But just as we were let out of our final classes, Megan managed to corner me near her locker. The loud buzz of kids near us built a bubble around our conversation.

"I hear you hung out with Marie this weekend," she said. "How was that?"

"Fine," I said, "we went to a show at the Reverb."

"Ugh, that place is so gross. I went there once, remember, when I was dating Jason and he had that awful nu-metal band? The whole place smelled like—well, anyway, I just wanted to let you know what people are starting to say about you. I mean, I hate that they're talking behind your back, but if there's a reason they're saying what they are, I just thought you'd, like, want to know."

"What exactly are you trying to tell me here?"

"About you and Marie. What they're saying."

"Yeah?"

"Well, like, the word is that she's bi. And they say that she's trying to, like, seduce you or whatever. So it's probably good that you guys aren't talking much at school, but if you keep hanging out on weekends they're never going to shut up about it. And anyway, isn't she kind of weird? Like, she's so intense with not drinking and everything. How can you stand her?"

"Who's saying this stuff? How did anyone even hear about me and Marie?"

"You know how these things go," said Megan. Of course I knew. Too well.

"I mean, I'm not, we're not—it's not like we're dating or anything. I'm straight, obviously. You know that. I just wanted to go to this concert and we sort of went together. It wasn't a big deal or anything."

"I'm just saying, you better watch her. I know you can't control yourself around anyone who throws you, like, the slightest compliment or whatever."

"Hey," I said, "I thought you were over this."

"It still hurts, you know. And you running off and playing dyke doesn't make me feel any better."

Dyke. The total venom of that word. Like I had killed someone, like I had done something awful.

"Shut up, okay? It's none of your business. I'm not a—" The venom, that word, I couldn't say it. "God, don't you have prom committee now or something?"

"Okay, you need to calm down," she said. "And I know you're making fun of me, but I actually do have a prom committee meeting to get to. I'll see you around, Kat."

With my backpack on, I wandered through the school's front foyer. A bunch of different clubs had set up tables to raise money for different charities. It was some contest they were having or something, which seemed totally offensive because it was like people were only donating money for these causes to help their friends win a free pizza lunch. I could feel the bill, the red bill, throbbing in my wallet even through the wall of textbooks and gym clothes that filled my bag.

"Hey," said a guy in a long-sleeved polo shirt, "if you donate five dollars today to UNICEF, we'll give you this free pen!"

"No, no, no," said a girl at the table next to him, "come over here, the French Club is raising money for the Humane Society. We've got pictures of puppies, and cupcakes for anyone who donates a toonie."

"Over here!" someone else called, but I didn't even turn around to see who was yelling. "Doctors Without Borders needs your support. And so does the basketball team!"

My face turned as red as Mackenzie King's—the man on the guilty fifty—and I got out of there as fast as I could.

Marie broke her vow of silence later that night and called around nine.

"Hi," she said, "Kathy?"

My face was hot.

"Yeah," I said, "hey."

"So. You bailed pretty fast the other night."

"You were kind of ignoring me and Chantal. Plus I felt sick."

"It was really lame for you to ditch me to drink with Chantal's sketchy friend, you know. Oh yeah, and she told me you guys made out. He said you started acting really weird 'cause you were so drunk and that's why he left."

"I was just a little buzzed," I said. "He pretty much forced himself on me; it was pretty gross. So I turned him down, he called me a bitch and then he left."

"Oh, shit," she said. "Seriously? I'm so sorry. Chantal didn't tell me any of that."

"She didn't know. It's not like Ivan was going to tell her what really happened, so he obviously lied to save face about it."

"But that's so wrong, why didn't you tell us what happened?"

"Because I didn't want to talk about it. And I don't want to talk about it now, either."

"Sorry," she said, "that's so not okay for him to act like that. That's disgusting. I'm totally going to call him out the next time I see him."

"Please don't, I don't want to make this into some big thing."

"What, so he can keep raping girls in parking lots?"

"He didn't—I mean, it definitely didn't get that far. And he did leave when I told him to. But I felt pretty awful afterwards. I don't know, maybe you're right, you should call him out. But for now, can we please change the subject?"

"Okay, we don't have to talk about it right now. It was still lame that you were drinking, though."

"I'm not straight edge," I said, "I never told you I was."

"I know, but drinking's just so stupid. It's like, I could have a great night and go to a show and see a band I love and make a new friend and dance and have an amazing time, and I don't need a drop of booze to do it. So why even bother with trying to get strangers to buy it for you and then acting like an idiot and having a hangover the next day? It just seems so pointless."

"And that works for you. Good."

"I just think it's stupid," she said.

"Fine, think whatever you want."

"So, hey," she said, palpably switching back into Marie Before This All Happened mode. "I got Josie's email address. She said she wants to hear my band when we can record something and she'll get us on a bill with Falter, isn't that cool?"

"Wasn't there some other band that was going to get you guys on a bill, too?" I asked, remembering the conversation I'd overheard in the falafel shop the week before.

"Yeah," she said, "hopefully. Mostly I just use the whole I-have-a-band, you-should-let-us-open-for-you line on any musicians I talk to. It doesn't hurt to get your name out there and make friends."

"That sounds kind of sleazy. Isn't that, like, schmoozing or whatever?"

"It's not. I just happen to know that if there's one thing in the world that I could love for my whole life and want to do every day and completely dedicate all of my energy and my time and my love to, it's music. Playing music. And this is what I have to do."

"Wow," I said, "I didn't realize you were so driven."

Where did that drive come from? How could Marie know herself so well? I felt like such a stranger to myself. I hardly even knew what I liked anymore; without Megan around to tell me what to buy, what to watch and what to wear, I barely knew who I was.

"That's the plan," she said. "And once we graduate we'll have so much time to focus and really get some good songwriting done."

"Cool, at least you've got a plan."

"Yeah. Hey, do you want to come to band practice? I think we're having one on Thursday after school. I can't believe I haven't introduced you to Macy and Jacque yet. I'm really sorry for acting so grumpy today and ignoring you and everything, I didn't know that Ivan was being so horrible. Let me make it up to you, come meet my friends."

"Sure," I said, "okay. I'd like that."

"Oh, and I forgot to tell you, but your mix tape's almost done. You still want it, right?"

"Yeah, thanks for doing that. I can't wait to hear it."

"Cool," she said, "cool. I'll see you tomorrow."

In bed that night I got out one of my old notebooks that I kept in the drawer of my bedside table. I made a list of some of the things that my grandma had loved doing. I thought that maybe I could find something in the list, some hint about what to do so that I could remember her, always, but to be able to move on. And to get rid of that guilty money that I still hadn't done anything good with. That I hadn't done anything with at all.

Money was never important to Grandma. Sure, she'd had more of it than most people, but she didn't show it off. She wrote cheques for charity, but she gave her family—she gave me—her time, her undivided attention. She knew that was what was really valuable. My life felt important when she listened to me. Every tiny accomplishment meant more when I told her about it and when she told me how proud she was.

I wrote down small things she loved, anything I could remember. Knitting and reading, writing, painting, travelling, playing cards and cooking. But nothing I wrote down seemed big enough. I wanted to make a grand gesture. Something to give people hope. Hell, something to give myself hope. I wanted to say something to everyone walking around with their eyes shut to the world, something about how we never really have enough time with the people in our lives who've helped make us what we are, but that we have to be able to live the way they taught us.

It was too late at night, and the words were sliding together and bumping into each other in my mind. I thought about Ivan again and his salty tongue, about all the stupid, awful things Megan said and how she seemed to mean every one.

I squeezed out a few tired and frustrated tears, hating myself for not being able to focus on the money, on the good and on Grandma. I looked down at the notebook again. I wrote: *bake sale for charity*. I grimaced at my handwriting and then crossed it out. I wrote: *volunteer at a homeless shelter*. Then I circled the word volunteer until I'd blotted it out completely. I wrote: *paint a mural somewhere (community centre?)*. Then I scratched out the word mural, too, after I'd sketched out a few sickly looking stick figures on another piece of paper. Definitely not.

I tried to remember the last time I'd felt good. Really good.

Not just lying-in-my-room-alone-with-a-CD-on-good, but loved-completely-by-another-person-good. Safe-good. Happy-good. And, of course, it was before she died. And I didn't know if I'd ever stop waking up every day and feeling like I was alone, and even when I'm with other people I'm alone, and maybe I'm the kind of person who's always going to be alone.

There were a few more tears and then there was sleep.

In my dream, Marie tried to hold my hand, but hers was concrete and mine was slime and we couldn't make it work.

I woke up then and went to the bathroom. I went back to bed, hoping hard for no more dreams. Hoping that in the morning I would remember nothing.

On Thursday, Megan found me at my locker after school. "You're not still hanging out with Marie are you?" she asked. "Because someone in my French class said they heard she's getting you to, like, play drums in her band or something."

"I'm just going to watch them practise," I said. "Why's it such a big deal?"

"I just thought that if you were going to ditch me for someone, you'd at least do it for someone who was cool."

"You ditched me first," I said. "When you and Pat got together it was like I never existed. Actually, you know what? No. It was a long time before that. It was when you started dating Jason, and then Mark. It's like you haven't been single for two weeks since you hit puberty, and as long as you have a guy around you don't need me. You ditched me first."

"I think you know that's not how it happened." Her face didn't move. She looked like a robot. This was the girl who

I'd played Barbies with for weekends at a time. How had we become such strangers? "Jack's coming home this weekend. He asked about you, and now my mom's making me invite you to dinner."

"He's back?" I said. "For how long?"

"He's just in for the weekend, then he's going back to university. So are you going to come to dinner?"

"Yeah, I guess so. I mean, I feel weird saying no."

"Whatever, do what you want."

"Can I let you know tomorrow?"

"Fine," she said, "just tell me by Friday if you're coming."

I left the building and met up with Marie and her friends. They were standing a ways off from the front door, and Marie was facing the other way, but even with a hundred kids between us fighting to catch their buses home, I found the back of her head—spiked out and freshly dyed black—in the crowd, as if there was a giant arrow pointing to her.

"Hey," I called out when I got closer.

"Hey, Kath!" she said, turning to face me and then bringing me into the circle her friends had formed. "This is Jacque," she said, pointing to Shawarma Girl, "and this is Macy," pointing to Girl Number Three, who held a soft guitar case in one hand and a small amp in the other.

"Hey," I said. "So where do you guys practise?"

"We used to play at my house," Jacque said, "but it was bugging my mom that we were there so much, making so much noise, so now we rotate between houses. Which is a huge pain in the ass because it means dragging my drum kit around every time we want to play."

"I told you we should talk to her about investing in some sound insulation," Marie said. "It wouldn't be so bad if the noise were muffled a bit."

"Yeah, sure, I'll work on that," Jacque said sarcastically. "In the meantime, I have to go home, borrow my parents' car, load up the drums and come meet you guys at Marie's."

"Are your amps working?" Macy asked. "I really don't want to get shocked again. I brought my tiny amp just in case."

"They're fine," Marie said. "They'll be totally fine for today." Then she turned to me and said, "Okay, so no one else other than us has heard the band yet, so you have to be totally objective and tell us what you think. Oh, and I can give you your mix tape! I finished it last night, I just forgot to bring it to school."

"Sure," I said, "I can do honest."

"Fine," Jacque said, "so are you guys all heading over to Marie's now? I'll be there in an hour."

"An hour?" said Marie. "We'll hardly have any time to

practise before eight o'clock."

"What happens at eight?" I asked.

"Marie's neighbours become totally unreasonable," said Macy. "We have to turn it down at eight."

"Hey, at least my mom and stepdad don't mind the noise," Marie said. "Anyway, we better get going if we want to play at all tonight."

Marie, Macy and I walked to Bathurst station and then took the subway a few stops west to Lansdowne. We walked south for a couple of blocks until we got to Marie's house.

"It's kind of messy in here," she said. "My parents are trying to, like, renovate or something, but it just looks kind of awful right now." She took her key chain out of her backpack and fit one of the three keys on the ring into the door. "Don't worry about taking your shoes off or anything," she said, "my parents don't care." We took off our slushy boots anyway, leaving them on a mat by the door. The house was totally normal-looking, but Marie kept acting weird, nervous. She was talking even faster than usual, her words were barely intelligible.

"Do you guys want some snacks or something? We don't have anything great right now, but we've got, like, cheese and crackers and stuff, is that okay? There's some pop in the refrigerator, too, I think."

We nodded that it was fine and grabbed a couple of cans of pop out of the fridge. Marie got out a block of cheese, a cutting board and a knife. She kept on talking too fast as she sliced into the cheddar, and I was worried she'd have a tough time playing guitar with only four fingers.

"Uh, Marie?" I said, cutting off her story about how great her mom's meatloaf was, but how she couldn't eat it anymore since she had gone vegetarian six months before. "Is everything okay?"

"What? Yeah, no, it's fine. I guess I just get a bit nervous having friends over. My mom's this mega-hostess, and I just want my friends to feel comfortable."

"I've been here, like, twenty times," Macy said. "You don't have to be nervous about me."

They both turned to look at me. "What?" I said, "Is this because I'm here? Your house is great. I think you just need to take it down a couple of notches, you know?"

"Yeah, sure," she said, "thanks for saying that. But you must be used to places way nicer than this."

"What's that supposed to mean?" I asked.

"You are kind of a rich kid," Macy said. "I mean, it's not that you're snobby or anything, but everyone knows who your mom is."

"She's such a great reporter," Marie said. "She's just so

poised and confident and so, so smart. It must be really cool to live with her."

"Yeah," I said, "when she's around." I stopped. I'd shared too much. Somehow I wanted Marie to know everything. Was that crazy? "Whatever, we're not loaded or anything. I mean, yeah, our house is kind of fancy, but I really don't think of us as being, you know, rich. I think your house is great. It looks like people actually live here." And it did. It was a whole other kind of home.

"Oh," she said, "okay. Thanks for saying that. I just was thinking to myself, 'Shit, what's Kathy going to think of the house? It's so small and it's so messy and'—well, anyway, I was definitely overthinking it."

"Is it Kathy or Katherine?" Macy asked. "Or is it Kath?"

"No one ever really calls me Kathy, or Kath, other than Marie. I get Kat sometimes, too. I don't know, it doesn't make much difference. Call me what you want."

"Okay," she said, "I'll try to figure out what suits you."

Not long after that, Jacque rang the doorbell. "You've all gotta help me move this stuff," she announced on the front step, "it's heavy as hell. My mother didn't want me driving it all around in her brand new soccer mom mobile, but she finally gave in after, like, a year of begging and pleading and promising to do the dishes."

The four of us went out to the street, where Jacque had parked her mom's car. She gave me an armload of cymbal stands and I followed her, Marie and Macy back into the house and down into the basement. There were a couple of amps plugged into a power bar in the corner and a microphone that looked like it might be a kids toy was mounted on a stand in the middle of the room.

"Just put those stands down over here," Jacque said, "it'll take me a few minutes to put everything together."

I sat down on the couch that faced where the girls were setting up and watched them tune, test their amps and cords, and put the pieces of Jacque's drum set together—tasks that were totally foreign to me. I recognized their tools, but felt like an alien as I watched them move so comfortably around each other and their instruments. They knew how to put it all together—what to plug in where, which knobs to turn— and I had no idea. They moved like rock and roll machines, designed to do bizarre, minute tasks that it seemed like no human could ever manage. I stared at Jacque as she meticulously moved her floor tom back and forth, adjusting it in relation to her bass and snare drums. She gave her kick pedal a tentative thump thump, then, seeming satisfied, started putting her cymbals onto their stands. When I thought about it, I realized that I'd seen musicians set up like this before, of course I had. I'd seen guys with wild hair set up giant amplifiers on stage in front of an anxious crowd of people, but this was totally different. When I'd seen bands play before it always seemed so out of reach and impossible. But here was Marie's band, right in front of me, ready to take chances and make some noise without anyone's request or permission.

"How did you talk your parents into buying you a drum set?" I asked.

"I played in the jazz band in middle school," Jacque said. "They bought me a used kit a few years ago, but I've bought some new cymbals and stuff since then."

Marie and Macy passed a tuner back and forth, trying to get to the same key. "So, does one of you play bass?" I asked.

"No," said Macy, "we both play guitar. I think I started learning first, but then Marie wanted to start a band and she said she absolutely wouldn't play bass."

"It just seemed so obvious to be a girl playing bass," Marie said. "Like, okay, I know Kim Deal makes it look good—"

"—Kim Gordon, too," said Jacque.

"Yeah, the Kims make playing bass look great and cool," said Marie, "but it's just such a rock band cliché, and we want to be more unique than that."

"Is it still cliché to have a girl bass player if you're all girls?" I asked without a trace of sarcasm.

Jacque gave me an unimpressed look.

"Well, whatever, bass is boring," Marie said. "I wanted to play guitar." They finished setting up and Marie looked at her watch. "It's almost six," she said. "Let's make some noise while we still can."

And then they made their noise. It was hard to tell if they had any real songs at all. Macy sort of whined into the mic, while she and Marie strummed chords that were still somehow way off despite their efforts to tune. Jacque's drumming was taut, and each time she brought her stick down on a drum or a cymbal it punched through the haze of guitars and hit me in the middle of my forehead. They played—starting and stopping every few minutes—for an hour. Macy did this thing where she closed her eyes when she sang, even when they were just improvising, and she was making the words up as they came to her. Marie bit lightly on her tongue and stood almost tip-toe on her right foot, staring intently at her instrument. I realized after a while that I was staring at her mouth. Her chapped lips and her tongue between her teeth.

When they had finally exhausted their ideas, they turned off the amps and crowded around me on the couch.

"So, what do you think?" Marie asked. "I know we're pretty rough, and I think maybe our guitars sort of fell out of tune after a while, but it sounded all right, right?"

"It was interesting," I said.

"That sounded sincere," said Jacque.

"No," I said, "I just mean, it's hard to describe your sound because it's so unique and everything."

"Okay," said Marie, "but what did you actually think of it. Like, did you like it?"

"I—it's really challenging music."

"You can just say you didn't like it," Macy said. "Our music is very personal, I get that not everyone's going to like it, it's not a big deal."

"No—it kind of reminded me of some other stuff. It sounded good. Like, with a bit more practise, you guys could be opening for, like, Falter."

"Yeah," Jacque said, "with a bit more practise." She walked back to her drum set and started taking her cymbals off their stands.

"What are you doing?" Marie asked.

"I'm going home," Jacque said. "You want to help me pack this stuff up?"

"But it's only a bit after seven," she said

"Whatever," Jacque said, pissed. "I've got a lot of homework to do. Since we won't all be quitting our day jobs any time soon."

"That isn't what I meant," I said, high-voiced, whiny, too

apologetic, "You guys are twisting my words. I liked your band. I like your band. Why are you being so sensitive?"

"It's very personal music," Macy said again, unplugging her guitar and putting it back into its case.

"Come on," Marie said, "you guys should stay for dinner. We'll probably order Thai food or something, it'll be great."

"Sorry, Marie," Macy said, "but I should probably get home too. Jacque? Can you give me a ride?"

"Sure," she said, "just help me carry this stuff back upstairs."

Macy and Jacque loaded the van back up and took off without saying much else or offering me a lift home.

"I'm sorry about that," said Marie, when they'd left. "I know you didn't mean to upset them."

"I really liked the way you guys sounded. I thought it was great. I can't believe they thought I was insulting them. I just have a hard time talking about music, and you guys really don't sound like anything I've heard before."

"Oh. Well, originality's never a bad thing. Anyway, they'll get over it eventually," she said, "I'll tell them you really did like us. Hey, do you want to go listen to your mix tape in my room?"

I thought about going home. It wouldn't be too far to walk, though it was cold outside. I still had the cab card, too, so I could be home pretty quickly. Eating dinner alone, reading and watching bad TV. There was cereal in the cupboard, though it was possible that that was the only edible thing left in the house. Froot Loops, and milk that was probably past its expiry date. "Sure," I said, "lead the way."

Marie's room looked just like I'd expected it to: it was like a natural extension of her wardrobe and her personality thrown up on four small walls. She sat down on her bed and picked up what I assumed was my tape.

"See?" she said. "I was so close to getting it into my bag this morning. But then I started looking through one of my old yearbooks, and then by the time I looked at my watch again I was totally late, so I had to rush and then I just forgot to bring it with me. But anyway, here it is."

She handed me the tape's case and I turned it over in my hands. She'd made a collage cover and cut out tiny letters from a magazine to spell out *Ms. Boatman's Wild Ride*. "Wow," I said, "this looks amazing."

"Do you get it?" she asked. "Like *Mr. Toad's Wild Ride*? You know, at Disney World? I wasn't sure if it was too weird or obscure or something."

"No," I said, "I got it." I opened the case and unfolded a track list for the tape with lyrics that Marie had written out by hand.

"Whoa," I said, "this must have taken forever."

"I really love making mix tapes," she said. "Do you want to listen to it now? I really hope you'll like it, but maybe you'd rather just listen to it on your own and then you won't be worried about what I think or about me misunderstanding what you mean if you tell me you like it. I mean, if you like it."

"It's fine," I said, a little freaked by her efforts, but amazed that she'd spent so much time thinking about me. In a flash of a second I remembered the dream of our hands, concrete and slime. "Let's put it on."

Marie took the tape from the case—clear plastic that she'd painted purple on the back and the sides with what looked like nail polish—put it in her tape deck and pressed "play."

The first thing I heard was a dull drum beat, joined by a guitar. "I love Sonic Youth," Marie said, "I had to put them on first." The ten or so songs she'd recorded on the first side piled gracefully on top of each other, while Marie lay on her bed making comments every so often about a perfect riff or an amazing lyric. I was lying on the rug on the floor beside her, on my back, staring at the spots on her ceiling. It was a beautiful hypnosis. I just lay there, and after a while I could hardly feel the floor underneath me or Marie's chatter over the songs. I just focused on the unwinding magnetic ribbon in the tape deck and blocked out every other thing in the world.

"Do you like it?" she asked when we heard the click at the end of the side.

"It's great," I said, "I really do. I like it a lot."

"Want to hear side two?"

"Absolutely."

She got up from the bed, hit "eject" and flipped the tape over. "The first song on this side is kind of important," she said. "I was thinking it could be, like, your theme song."

I reached for the track listing to see what the song was called: "The Boat Dreams from the Hill."

"Ha," I said, "Boat, Boatman. I get it."

"It's so much more than that," she said. And then she hit "play".

Again, the drums were the first thing I heard, tumbling out this time, followed closely by an anxious guitar.

"Read the lyrics," Marie said. "Blake's such a great writer."

"Blake?" I asked. "You mean like the poet? 'Tyger, tyger, burning bright' and all that?"

"No, different guy. Blake Schwarzenbach, he's the singer."

"What's the band called?" I asked, looking for their name in the lyric notes.

"Jawbreaker," she said. "They're so great." And she sang

along, even though the words kind of ran together and didn't really sound like how she'd written them out. The chorus went something like: "I wanna be a boat, want to learn to swim, then I'll learn to float and then begin again." It was a fun song, but it obviously didn't mean as much to me as it did to Marie.

She rewound the tape and we played the song five times over. I mumbled the verses from my little lyric sheet, while Marie determinedly sang her articulations over top, and we joined together for the chorus.

"I wanna be a boat, want to learn to swim, then I'll learn to float and then begin again."

We both stood up and started dancing around the room. We were jumping and throwing our hair around, raising our arms in the air and shaking like fundamentalists in the face of God. I didn't really understand the lyrics, but by the fifth time through I felt them. The pummelling guitars and the gruff wistfulness of the singer's delivery made me want to pound my fists on my chest loud enough to piss off the neighbours. It was incredible. Two and a half perfect minutes.

We both collapsed on the floor when the song ended again, and Marie pushed herself up on one arm and turned to look at me. "You're really amazing, you know that?" she said.

"Thanks," I said.

"No, really. It's like you've been one person for so long and now you're finally letting yourself see this totally different side that you never thought existed. You're like—"she laughed, "—you're like hanging out with a butterfly."

I had no idea what to say, so I just said thanks again.

"No," she said, with this look in her eyes kind of like the one Ivan gave me in the parking lot right before his salty, orange tongue was in my mouth. "Really. Really, really. You're wonderful."

I wanted to run and stay perfectly still at the same time, to get the hell out of there and to climb up on the bed with her.

Fear won out.

"I better get going," I said, sitting up fast.

"Come on," she said, "stay for dinner. We can order anything you want. Chinese? Do you like Chinese food? Or Indian?"

"No, really," I said. "I forgot my mom said she was going to make dinner tonight. She'll be pissed I'm coming home so late."

"Oh. Well if you wait another half hour or so for my mom to come home I bet she can give you a ride. It'll save you some time, and we can finish listening to the tape."

"It's fine," I said, "I'll take a cab. It's no problem."

"Okay," she said, disappointed but resigned. "If you've really gotta go." She pressed "eject" on her tape deck, put the tape back into its case and handed it to me. "Don't forget this."

"Thanks," I said. Downstairs, I stuck the tape in my backpack, put on my big sweater and my coat and walked up to Bloor to hail a cab.

"See you tomorrow, Boat!" Marie called from the doorway.

"Yeah," I said. "I'll see you."

9

I got to school early the next day and on my way to English found Megan and Pat cuddling by Megan's locker with their textbooks spread out in front of them.

"Hey," I said.

"Hi," said Megan.

Pat nodded.

"So, I think I'll take you up on your invitation," I said. "To dinner, I mean. I'd like to come."

"Okay," she said, "that's fine. It's tomorrow. We usually eat at around seven."

"Yeah, I remember."

"So come over around six or six-thirty."

"All right," I said, "sounds good. Can I, you know, bring anything?"

"I'm sure you being there will be more than enough." Fake sweet. With venom.

I said goodbye and let them go back to their boning up. I decided to head to class early since the room was pretty much guaranteed to be deserted. Grayson was at his desk when I got there, revising his lesson plan and tapping out a steady rhythm with his loafers on the floor.

"Good morning, Katherine," he said.

"Morning, Mr. Grayson."

"I don't think I saw your assignment in the pile I was grading last night. I must have lost it somewhere, I'm sorry about that. Would you mind printing it out and submitting it again?"

"Oh, no, I didn't do it, sir. I couldn't, uh, finish it." I couldn't even remember what assignment he was talking about. I hadn't managed to finish any of the homework I'd been assigned in the last two weeks.

"That's very unlike you," he said. "Is everything all right?"

"No," I said, "but I don't really feel like talking about it. Could I have an extension on that paper? Just until Monday?" As if I'd be able to remember what it was and finish it by then. I was too much of a coward to just ask him to tell me what I was supposed to do. I'd have to get the instructions from one of my classmates.

"That's no problem, really, no problem." He smiled that totally pitying adult smile that I'm sure they have whole classes on in teachers college. "But are you sure there's nothing you'd like to talk about? Not necessarily to me, but we do have a guidance department. Do you know Ms. Barthelme? She's pretty cool, you might like talking to her."

"Thanks, I'll think about it."

He went back to his lesson plan, and I took *In the Skin of a Lion* out of my bag, rereading some of the passages I was having trouble understanding. Before long the rest of the class started arriving, and then it was nine o'clock and "O Canada" played over the intercom and we all stood up at our desks. And then it was over and we all sat down, and then someone from student council read the announcements, and then that was over and Mr. Grayson stood up.

"Today," he said, "I'd like to begin by talking more about the Bloor Viaduct since it figures so prominently in *In the Skin of a Lion*. Can anyone tell me what major decision was made regarding the bridge two years ago?"

No one put up their hand.

"No one?" he asked. "Okay. Well, let's think about all the ways that a stunning, historically-rich bridge can be used."

"Oh shit," James The Jock said, "it's a suicide thing, right?"

"Correct," Grayson said. "Since the Viaduct was completed in 1918, it's become something of a magnet for people who wish to end their lives."

"That's so sad," one of the girls said.

"Yes," Grayson said, "it's very sad. Two years ago, city council approved a plan to build what would effectively be a suicide barrier around the bridge. Does anyone remember hearing about this?"

There were a few nods of agreement and some oh yeahs.

"So, are they building it or what?" James asked.

"There's been a lot of discussion about how to fund the project and how much it's going to cost," Grayson said. "But what do you all think about building a barrier around the bridge? Will it deter suicides? Does it compromise the history of the Viaduct?"

"I think it's a good idea," James said, "they should spend as much money as they can on it. If people are going to be stupid enough to kill themselves, they shouldn't have such a cool place to do it."

Grayson didn't look convinced. "Would you mind explaining your point further?" he asked.

"Sure," James said. "I mean, it's selfish to kill yourself. You get to take the easy way out, while all your family and friends have to deal with it afterwards, it's not fair."

"Yes," Grayson said, "that's a very good point. But do you think that building this barrier will prevent people from committing suicide in Toronto?"

"Yeah," he said, "I think so. I think a lot of people who want to kill themselves do it sort of on impulse, like if they're having a really, really shit day." Grayson winced at his language. "If they went to the Viaduct to jump and found out they couldn't, maybe they'd decide not to do it."

"I doubt it," I said quietly.

"Yes, Katherine?" said Grayson.

"People who decide that their lives are awful enough that they don't want to live them anymore aren't just going to stop hating themselves if they put a wall up around the bridge. If it was me, I'd probably feel even worse if I got all the way out there and found out I couldn't jump. It's a simplistic way to try to solve something that's so much more complicated than we know. It sounds like they're just trying to save the city's reputation for the sake of our tourists." I was as surprised as anyone to hear the words come out of my mouth. I'd never really considered it before, but the thought came out of me fully formed. Like the feeling had been in me all along without my ever realizing it. Like in some strange light suicide made sense.

"Look out," one of the other gym guys said, "Katherine's going to jump!"

There was some general laughter, but Grayson cut in. "Not funny," he said in a way that only sounds like a good comeback when it's from the mouth of someone who's already lived through their adolescence. "Does anyone know what the proposed name for the barrier is?" Grayson asked when we'd all calmed down a bit. No one answered. "The Luminous Veil."

What total PR bullshit.

And then the bell rang for our next class and we all picked up our stuff to go.

After school, Marie came and found me at my locker. "Hey," she said, "sorry if I weirded you out yesterday. I mean, I know people talk a lot about me and I know they say that I'm a lesbian and everything and, you know, we haven't talked about any of this stuff before, and maybe I came on a bit strong yesterday. I just wanted to clear things up so it doesn't make our friendship weird or anything."

"Oh," I said, "I don't—I mean, I didn't know people said that."

"Sure you did, everyone knows. And I am. A lesbian, I mean. I like girls."

She was so calm. She said the words like they were completely normal. Like dry, scientific facts.

"That's—wow," I said, feeling my tongue grow too big for my mouth, "that's cool that you're so open about it." How could she be so open about it? How could she be so calm?

"I feel, like, really lucky to be one of those people who just knows exactly who they are when they wake up in the morning. It's kind of rare, supposedly. And, I mean, sometimes it does change from one morning to the next. I mean, god, I used to like ska!"

"But you're sure you are?" I asked. "Aren't you, I don't know, kind of young to just know that about yourself?"

"Nope," she said. "It's been pretty clear all along. Well, first I came out as bi, but after a little while of that it was pretty clear to me that guys weren't in the picture, like, at all. And it felt so good to be able to say that to myself. But anyway, I just wanted to make sure that you didn't think I was hitting on you or anything yesterday. I think you're so great, but I don't want you to feel uncomfortable around me and I don't want you to feel like there's anything you don't know about me. Anything you want to know, ever, just ask. I just hate lies and people who feel the need to tell them, you know? The world's screwed up enough, let's just try to be honest."

"So," I said, trying my best to be honest about my curiosity, "have you had, like, girlfriends?"

"Nothing really serious yet. I'm pretty choosy when it

comes to people I hang around with and people I date."

"Yeah," I said, "me too." Or at least I'd like to be, I thought.

"So, do you want to come over this weekend? There's another show, at the Kathedral this time, and I think you'd like it. Jacque and Macy want to come, too, so I thought we could all go to the show and then stay over at my house afterwards or something. You know, like a sleepover. It'll be great."

"When? Tomorrow night?"

"Yeah," she said, "sorry for the short notice. But can you come?"

"I'm having dinner with some, uh, some people, but I could probably meet you guys at the show. Would that be okay?"

"Yeah, absolutely. Amazing! This'll be so much fun."

"But are Jacque and Macy still pissed at me?" I asked.

"Don't worry, I'll talk to them before tomorrow night."

"Okay," I said, "if you're sure."

"I told you, I'm picky about my friends. I know you guys'll all get along eventually."

"Sure, sounds good. Oh, and I need to give you back your Falter CD."

"Right," she said, "can you bring it tomorrow? That would be great."

"Yup, no problem."

"Cool, I'll see you soon."
"Yeah," I said, "bye."

Marie was gay. A lesbian.
Marie was Marie.
Marie was too much too close too soon.
Marie was really something.

10

I spent most of Saturday afternoon freaking out about having to go over to the Whidden's for dinner. And trying not to think about Marie and her words. Her matter-of-fact-ness. Her hands.

On top of the fact that Megan had been acting so strange at school, I hadn't seen Jack since August. He'd been home for Christmas, but things were still so uncomfortable then between me and Megan that I couldn't call. Plus he hadn't emailed me at all during his fall term at Guelph. Because why should you bother to keep in touch with someone just because you had sex a couple of times and kind of dated? Even if the dating was behind your sister's back because you thought it would freak her out that you were into her best friend. Even when your younger sister was fifteen months younger and her best friend was only eleven months younger than you.

But it wasn't the age thing that was the problem, it was the my-younger-sister's-best-friend thing. Which was so stupid and awful because I loved Jack like a friend and not really like a boyfriend. But he was so into me and he'd gotten me into so much cool music and so many interesting books that when he called me late one night and asked if I'd like to take a walk with him, how was I going to say no? And I really respected him, and even though I wasn't really hot for him or anything, he was so cute, so charming and so kind, and of course I should have been into him, even though Megan totally hated the thought of us together, which I only brought up in a joking way to test the waters of actually telling her. She flipped at the hint, so we kept it a secret the rest of the summer until he had to leave for school.

And he said he wouldn't forget me for some university girl. And I didn't believe him. And he said that what we had was special. And I didn't believe him. And he said I was such a beautiful and good person that we fucked. I mean, we had sex. He tried to call it "making love," but I wouldn't let him get the words out. It hurt the first time, but less and less the second and third. And I was surprised at how little I cared. About him, about the sex, everything. It was something I'd heard about so many times, had been told over and over again how big a deal it all was. But it wasn't. And then I felt crazy for not caring—abnormal. Wasn't this supposed to be every teen girl's worst nightmare? I just felt kind of relieved. I don't talk about it and I try not to think about it.

Jack thought about it a lot; he said he did. He said he'd email me and that he'd call. But then he didn't. And I was almost sort of relieved. Until Megan found out.

So, anyway, I was freaked.

At my mom's insistence—she was so glad I was going over to Megan's, she thought this was a sign I was finally over my whole depression thing—I brought a bottle of wine for Megan's parents. I rang their doorbell at six thirty-two, and Megan answered the door.

"Good," she said, a total ice queen. "I thought you were going to be late."

"You said six-thirty, didn't you?"

"I said six or six-thirty."

"Fine," I said, "sorry I'm late. I brought wine for your parents."

"Surprised you're willing to come with booze now that you're best friends with Little Miss Drug-Free."

"Leave Marie out of this," I said. "Can I come inside? It's freezing."

"Please," she said, stepping aside from the doorway. "June, Mom and Jack are in the living room. You can bring the bottle into the kitchen."

I took off my coat and boots at the door and walked into the kitchen, desperate to buy some time before seeing Jack. "Hi, Mr. Whidden," I called to Megan's dad where he stood fussing with a sauce on the stove.

"Hello, Kat. The rest of the party's in the living room, I believe. You better go join them."

"I, uh, come bearing wine," I said.

"Oh, terrific. Very thoughtful of your folks. Why don't you just set it down there on the counter?"

I put the bottle down, then walked through the dining room to where Jack, Megan, June and their mother were sitting.

"Hi," I said, taking a seat in an arm chair. "Nice to see you guys again."

"It's been too long," Mrs. Whidden said. And it had been. The Whiddens had practically been my second set of parents for a while. "How are you? I was so sorry to hear about your grandmother."

"What?" Jack said. "Your grandma died?"

"Yeah," I said, "New Year's Eve. It was, um, she had a heart attack."

"Oh man," he said, "I didn't know. I'm so sorry."

"And I'm so sorry we couldn't all be at the funeral," said Mrs. Whidden.

"I'm not," said June. "Dead people are creepy."

"June, that's a very rude thing to say," Mrs. Whidden said.

"Sorry," June said.

"It's okay," I said, "it's sad but I'm managing well enough. I mean, I miss her a lot. It feels like she must just be on vacation or something, like one of the cruises she was nuts about. It hasn't totally hit me yet that she's gone, I think."

"Of course, it must have been a huge shock," Mrs. Whidden said.

"It was pretty scary," I said.

"But how is everything going at school?" Mrs. Whidden asked. "We hear so little from Megan. Well, other than about the prom committee."

"Excuse me for participating in, like, school-sanctioned activities," Megan said.

"Are you on the committee?" Mrs. Whidden asked.

"No," I said, "I'm not really doing any after-school stuff this term. Just trying to keep my head down and finish, you know?"

"Yeah, when you're not going to punk shows at gross bars with your weird new friends," Megan said.

"Megan," said Mrs. Whidden, "June, what's gotten into you girls today?"

"Must be PMS or something," Megan said. "What's your excuse, Junie?"

June shrugged, looking confused.

"Seen anyone good?" Jack asked.

"Yeah," I said, "I saw Falter last weekend."

"Oh man, aren't they great?" he said.

"Their singer Josie's pretty amazing," I said.

"Yeah," Jack said, "for sure."

"Dinner is served!" Mr. Whidden called from the dining room.

"Terrific, said Mrs. Whidden. And we all got up from our places and took seats around the massive glass table in their dining room.

After school snack time had always been a gourmet affair at Megan's house when we were kids. Her dad was an amazing cook and for dinner he'd made homemade gnocchi with pesto I was sure he'd also made himself, and a baby spinach salad with walnuts, blue cheese and pear.

"Wow," I said as he came out and served us. "This looks amazing."

"Thank you," Mr. Whidden said. "Bet you're not eating this well in residence, eh, Jack?"

"Definitely not," he said with his mouth full of gnocchi.

"So, how come you're in town for the weekend?" I asked.

"Dentist's appointment," he said between forkfuls.

"Yeah," Megan said, "because I'm sure it's so hard to find someone who'll take your money and tell you to floss more in Guelph."

"I like Dr. Tanaka," he said. "Besides, how could I miss a home-cooked meal like this?"

"Gee," Megan said, "it seemed like you were doing fine without us all fall semester."

"I was busy," he said, "I already apologized for this at Christmas. So I was a little distant, it was my first term at school, get over it."

"I am," she said.

"Yeah, sure," he said, "it really seems like it."

"You guys are being weird," said June.

"Yes," said Mr. Whidden, "they are."

"Please," Mrs. Whidden said, trying to cut the sibling antagonism and giving her husband a look. "How are you parents?" she asked me.

"My dad's had some big merger, or maybe it's still happening. Anyway, he hasn't been around much. But I guess that's good for business or whatever."

"And your mom?" Mr. Whidden asked. "We watch her

show every night."

"Yeah, it's the same old, same old with her. Crazy schedule. Plus there's some rumour they're going to change some of her station's programming, which might mean she'd have to do an earlier show. Or maybe they're going to want someone younger, who knows?" It felt good to be this honest with them, like old times.

"I doubt they'll need someone younger," Mrs. Whidden said. "Your mom's new haircut looks fantastic. I was thinking of having mine done the same way."

"Just tell your hairdresser you want a Boatman," Megan said. "Only make sure they don't take too much off the top. You still need your brain."

"Is that some kind of crack?" Mrs. Whidden asked.

"Why would I joke about such an outstanding journalist?"

"What is with your attitude tonight?" Mrs. Whidden asked. "I thought we were inviting one of your closest friends to dinner. What's gotten into you?"

"You might ask what's gotten into Katherine," she said.

"And what's that supposed to mean?" said Mrs. Whidden.

"Gee, Kat, do you want to explain?" asked Megan.

I sat there, silent. I turned my gaze only slightly to try to gauge Jack's expression, but it was blank. "I think I better go," I said. "Thanks for your hospitality."

"You can't leave now," said Mr. Whidden. "I've made crème brûlée for dessert. It's your favourite, isn't it?"

"No," I said, "I'm sorry. I have to—I need to go, now. I'm sorry." And I pretty much ran back to the foyer and put my boots and coat back on as Mr. and Mrs. Whidden protested from the kitchen, June started singing some dumb pop song from the radio, and Megan and Jack—I assumed—kept their chairs warm around the table. "I'm sorry," I said one last time to no one in particular, just trying to fill the awful silence. "I've gotta go."

The Veil, I thought. The Luminous Veil. Get there before the Luminous Veil.

But I knew I didn't have the nerve. Megan's house was only a couple of blocks from mine, so I walked home. My feet moved fast beneath me, and the red flush from my cheeks was cooled by the bitter wind. I went straight up to my room when I got in—no sign of my parents—and had hardly stripped off my coat and heavy sweater before I lay down on my bed and started bawling.

Why did Megan even pretend to forgive me for lying to her if she was just going to dredge it up in front of her whole family? I felt like I'd walked into a live trap. Jack probably didn't want to see me at all; it was just some nasty plan she had to make me feel even worse about myself. I curled up in the fetal position on my bed as more full-body sobs took over. I could feel the bed, with its vintage metal frame, shaking and swaying underneath me.

I remembered the time when I was nine, when I'd come home crying after Megan and I had been fighting over something really stupid and petty, and Grandma was visiting—she stayed with us most of the time anyway when I was a kid, my parents were gone so much—and she'd been so gentle, but so pragmatic, and everything made sense when she talked about what I should do. And Megan and I made up and everything was okay again. But now I had no one to give me that kind of advice and no one who loved me as much as she had, and I was never going to have that again and it felt so awful and unfair and I kept crying and the bed kept shaking. And then I thought about the money that I still hadn't figured out what to do with. Because nothing seemed right. Nothing.

An hour or so later, the phone rang. I guessed that it was Marie and when the answering machine in the kitchen downstairs picked up the call I knew I was right. I could hear her too-loud voice from all the way upstairs.

"Hey," she said, "Kathy? Are you there? It's Marie. I just wanted to, you know, remind you about the show tonight at the Kathedral. Macy, Jacque and I are just about to leave if you still want to meet us there. Maybe your dinner thing ran long or something, I don't know, but I talked to the girls about practice and they totally understand that you didn't mean what you said as an insult. So, it's cool, and we'd really like to see you tonight. Anyway, we're leaving now, so we'll be at the Kathedral at around ten, which I think is when the first band is supposed to go on. They're called Royal Pain and they're supposed to be really great. They're, like, this drum and guitar girl duo and, anyway, I guess I've gotta go. But hopefully I'll see you tonight!"

About ten minutes passed before the phone rang again. Again, I let it ring to the machine. The voice wasn't as loud this time, but it still rang out through the silent house.

"Hey," Jack's voice said, "I'm calling for Kat. I just wanted to say that I'm sorry about dinner. I know Megan was being a pain in the ass, but I wasn't much better. Anyway, I'm only in town until tomorrow afternoon, but I was hoping we could talk, so—"

I picked up the phone. "Hey," I said. "Thanks, uh, thanks for calling."

"I'm really sorry," he said.

"Let's just not talk about it."

"I feel like I should make it up to you or something. Can

I buy you a coffee? Do you want to get together for a bit to-morrow before I leave?"

I'd finally stopped crying. I rubbed the fingers of my free hand over my eyelids. "Actually," I said, "what are you doing tonight?"

We met up not long after that on the streetcar platform at Bathurst. We got on without saying much. He asked me again who was playing that night, and we took turns staring out the window and at our feet. We got off at Queen Street and made our way inside the venue. I had smaller bills with me this time, but as I started to hand my five over to the guy working the door, Jack waved a hand at me.

"It's okay, I've got this," he said. He handed the guy at the cash box a ten and we each got our hands stamped. We sat down at one of the tables on the floor. Scanning the crowd, Jack said, "I can't believe I actually missed this place."

"Why?" I said. "It's not so bad."

The Kathedral was, I guess, a little bit smaller than the Reverb upstairs. It looked just as grungy, but it felt good to be there. My boots were heavy on the ground, like my feet belonged there. Not that it was saying much, but it was the best I'd felt all day.

"Come on," Jack said, "it's a dump. I'm not saying it's not great to have all-ages shows, it's so important to have a place like this, but once you turn nineteen you're going to realize that there are a lot of other, cooler places to go."

"Great," I said without enthusiasm. "So, did you tell Megan you were coming to meet me?"

"Why would I do that? You want me to make things worse between you two?"

"Well, you're still here."

"I know. And maybe I shouldn't be."

I could feel it, the dam of my mouth was about to break again.

"Look," I said, "I still feel awful about lying to Megan all summer about us sort of being together." His face showed nothing but guilt, so I switched tactics, reassuring him. "But, I mean, it's not like I still want you or anything. Really." He relaxed a bit. "I just, I don't know, you left without saying anything. And then you didn't try to keep in touch at all when you left for school. You made me feel like I trashed my friendship with Megan for nothing, you know?" Radical honesty. "That really sucked."

"I know," he said, "I'm sorry about that. It wasn't about you."

"Sure, it could have been anyone. But it was me. God, this really wasn't what I was planning on talking about with you tonight."

"What do you want to say? Whatever it is, I probably deserve it. Shoot."

"I don't know," I said. "I just feel so fucked up right now. And I don't think Megan and I are ever really going to be friends again. And I'm really pissed at you for never calling, I am. But, I mean, it's not what you think. Like, yeah, I had a lot of fun with you this summer. But, like, I don't have, you know, feelings for you anymore. I just—it felt like you deserted me as a friend. Like I wasn't cool enough for you to keep in touch with once you went off to university. And I miss you. I mean, as a friend. And I could really use a few more decent people in my life who I could actually talk to, you know? Could we just be friends again?"

"Yeah," he said, "that'd be good."

We sat there for a few minutes without saying anything else. But then I saw Marie across the room with Macy and Jacque, and I caught her eye and she came rushing over towards us.

"Hi," she said, wrapping her arms around me, "I'm so

glad you made it. Who's your friend?"

"This is Jack," I said.

"Hey," Jack said, "how's it going?"

"Good," she said, "so good. Did you guys just get here? You must've or I would've seen you before. You just missed Royal Pain, they were excellent. Kind of a Sonic Youth vibe, it was cool. So how was your dinner thing?"

"It sucked," I said. Jack smiled nervously. "But it's over now."

"Oh, one of those things," she said. "What happened? Do you want to talk about it? We can talk about it if you want to."

"No, not really." Silence. "Hey, Jack," I said, desperate to change the subject, "Marie here is in a band, they're pretty great."

"Oh yeah?" he said. "What do you play?"

"Guitar," she said, "just, you know, power chords mostly, but I think I'm getting a lot better. My bandmates are here, actually, Macy and Jacque—they're over there by the stage. Oh! I should go get them. Introduce Jack to Jacque, that would be so funny! Just wait here a sec."

Jack said, "She's a bit—"

"Intense?"

"Yeah."

"I know, but she's also about the only decent person I know right now. She's really sweet, you just have to sort of psych yourself up to have a conversation with her. She means well."

Marie returned with Macy and Jacque in tow. "Jack, meet Jacque," she said, giggling. "And this is Macy. Jacque's our drummer and Macy plays guitar, too, and she sings."

"No bassist?" Jack asked.

"We didn't want to fall into that girls playing bass stereotype," Marie said.

"Does that still count if you're all girls?" Jack asked.

"Whatever," Jacque said, "we like playing with two guitars."

"Cool," he said, "do you guys have a name?"

"We haven't been able to decide on one yet," Macy said. "Soon maybe, hopefully."

Jack excused himself to go buy a drink, and the second band of the night started setting up their gear on stage.

"Who are these guys?" I asked.

"They're called Stark," Marie said. "I haven't really heard them before but I know they're supposed to be pretty good. Seriously though, I think Royal Pain is going to be the highlight of the night for me. I just feel so good. I am so ready to make some music right now."

"Are you going to pull your amateur networking thing again?" Jacque asked. "You should maybe wait until we at least have a name for our band before you start whoring us out to every girl in a short skirt with a guitar." Not that she hadn't proven it already, but Jacque clearly wasn't one for tact. She tossed the words off casually, but they were still hateful.

"Shut up." Marie said. "What's going on with you? First you guys get pissed at Kathy when she hears us play, then you don't want me to talk to other bands to get us a show. Do you even want to be in the band?"

"Of course I do. But I hate that you keep pushing us to do things we aren't ready for. You keep talking to people like this band thing is already happening when we've only just started. We're still total beginners. It's like you're so impatient to be a rock star already that you don't care that we're not any good yet. You've got to let us get good first, before you start telling everyone how amazing we are, how we should open for them, inviting your friends to watch us practise so they can just insult us."

"I thought you guys were great," I said. "You took what I said totally the wrong way and then flipped out for no reason. And Marie's just trying to help get you guys off to a good start, she's doing her best. Give her a break."

"I think maybe this isn't your argument, Katherine," Macy said in this really level-headed and mature way that seemed totally impossible and was actually kind of annoying. "Maybe you should go catch up with your friend and leave this to us."

I said fine and went to go find Jack at the bar. He'd run into some girl he knew and they were talking and smoking, leaning in close because the music they were playing over the PA was so loud. I just stood there watching them for a minute, trying hard not to cry. Not about Jack, just about everything.

"I think I'm gonna go," I yelled into his ear after I willed myself to approach him. "My friends are fighting and I need to go home."

"Oh, that's too bad," he said. "You sure? You can hang out with me and Charlotte."

"No," I said, "no. I have to leave." What had happened to that belonging feeling, how had it managed to disappear so quickly?

"Okay, if you're sure. You want me to wait with you for the streetcar?"

"It's okay," I said, "I'm just going to get a cab. I've got my mom's card thing."

Jack got off his bar stool. He hugged me, and I didn't put my arms around him but I was glad to feel his warmth. "Email me, okay?" he said. "We can be, like, pen pals. Meg doesn't need to know."

"Sure," I said. "Okay." And I went out onto the street, hailed a cab, and went home. I cried the whole way.

The Veil. The Veil. The Veil.

11

It kept happening. This stupid, awful drama that followed me everywhere. It wasn't that I hadn't brought some of it on myself. Yes, I could have turned Jack down. Or yes, I could have just been honest with Megan when it—me and Jack, whatever we were—started happening. But I didn't, and I didn't.

I could have lied and said nicer things at Marie's band practice, or I could have just told her about how I think about her more than I should if she's just my friend. And how it scares the hell out of me that I think about her as much as I do, every night and every morning, even though when we're out together or when we're talking at school I'm still kind of afraid that someone will see us. Because she's so embarrassing, she talks so loud and she can be so preachy with her straight edge stuff and she's just too, too big. Her personality, her voice, her opinions, everything is just larger than any other person I've ever met. But I still want to talk to her and see her and listen to tapes in her bedroom. And other stuff, too, maybe. What would Grandma have to say about it if she was still here? Would she still have loved me if I was a... if I was... I don't know. I don't want anyone to know.

That maybe I'm really something, like Marie.

That I still dream about our hands.

That concrete and slime could never hold each other.

And even though I was pretty much over the fact that Megan and I had almost nothing in common anymore, it still hurt so badly, her being so mean. Especially her being so mean in the same house where we used to play Barbie's dream date while her dad made us lobster grilled cheese sandwiches. I knew she was hurt, was still hurting, that we'd been drifting so much and that I'd lied to her, had kept on lying. She knew that Jack and me being together was just the last piece of evidence that it wasn't the Megan and Kat Show anymore.

But of course, it wasn't about Jack. He was just there. His eyelashes and his CD collection and his drivers' license and his ticket out of town at the end of the summer. I think it doesn't matter whether you start in a small, rural town or in a city that prides itself on being world class. No matter what, you have the lust to leave because it doesn't seem special if it's just always been there. So Jack was kind, good-looking and liked good music. And he was leaving. And leaving was the only way I could see to get out of a drifting friendship, away from parents that existed more often on the TV than in the living room. Getting away from the emptiness of things— wealth, relationships, love, whatever. Nothing feels special when you have it all the time. So maybe the only way to make a life seem special is to cut it short. It seemed so perfect and so obvious. An inevitability, a perfect, symbolic solution.

Which is stupid, which is selfish, which is nothing Grandma would have ever found value in. Which can't be the way to be a good person. Which can't be anything. But it felt so tempting, so seductive. So simple and so definitive. Cutting it short.

So, on Sunday I took the subway out to Castle Frank station. Because Grayson had told us we really should go out and see the Viaduct for ourselves, if we hadn't already. Especially now, while it still existed the way it did in the novel. Before any veil, Luminous or otherwise, shaded the site. I brought the book with me. Grayson had proposed strolling the length of the bridge while reading the book aloud. The suggestion had solicited giggles, snickering and someone cough-yelling, "Queer!"

"If we walk on a bridge without looking where we're going, won't we, like, get hit by a car?" one of the girls asked. Grayson said it had only been a suggestion, a romantic ideal.

I didn't read while I walked. I walked silently past the Bell pay phone and the sign that read:

> DISTRESS CENTRE WE LISTEN
> 24 HOURS A DAY (416) 408-HELP (4357)

I watched the CN Tower poke out of the tops of the buildings and skeletal trees that lined the sides of the Viaduct. I noticed my breath fog the air in front of my face. I counted footprints in the snow in the Don Valley beneath me. And I stopped in the middle, with my hands braced on the stony barrier. And I pictured my body falling. The blast of air and the soft thud. I considered where to aim—the frozen river, or the Don Valley Parkway a hundred paces or so west. I breathed slowly and closed my eyes. I counted backwards from ten. I tried hard to get Grandma's face out of my mind, but I found myself thinking of Mackenzie King, the red bill.

I counted down again, from twenty this time. I imagined nothingness. Nothingness looked a lot like the Reverb the night Marie and I showed up before the crowd. I counted fifteen, fourteen, and kept breathing. I thought of Marie up on the stage, bending down to kiss me. Eleven, ten. I pictured us holding hands walking down the hall. Five, four. People laughing at us, shoving us, calling us names. My parents, crying, yelling. Two, one.

But I couldn't do it. Of course I couldn't. Did I really think I had the guts to throw myself off? How could I have been so stupid? How could I have been such a dumb coward?

I walked the rest of the length of the bridge, waited for a gap in traffic, crossed to the north side and walked back to Castle Frank. When I took my seat on the subway train, I could feel my whole body twitching, vibrating, alive with an electrical current I had never felt before. I fought to keep my knees from knocking against each other. From Castle Frank to Sherbourne. From Sherbourne to Yonge. From Yonge to Bay, and Bay to St. George. From St. George to Spadina. I couldn't stand up at Spadina, too afraid that I wouldn't be able to support my own weight. So I stayed on the train, riding to the end of the line in the west—Kipling station. I sat as still as I could as the rest of the passengers on the train got up to leave and more people replaced them, sitting in the seats that only minutes before had belonged to someone else, had supported them and still carried traces of their existence: their body heat, strands of their hair. The subway doors closed again and we rode back east. Passing Islington, passing Royal York, passing Old Mill, and Jane. Passing Runnymede, and High Park. Keele station, and Dundas

West. Lansdowne, Dufferin, Ossington, Christie, Bathurst, and then Spadina again. And when we arrived and my knees finally felt still and I was strong enough to stand, I got up and walked through the subway doors. And no one around me knew. No one knew that I'd already ridden past my stop once. That I couldn't stop my body from shaking and from thinking terrible, selfish things that I was afraid to even admit to myself. The drop from the bridge. The air that seemed cold enough to freeze a body as they jumped. I put my hands deep into the pockets of my coat and walked home.

12

Marie spent most of the next week at school fighting and negotiating with Jacque and Macy, while Megan gave me the silent treatment. I ate lunch alone in the bathroom and got a lot of reading done; anything to keep myself distracted. It was easier to eat in one of the toilet stalls, because it saved me from having to dash out of the cafeteria every time I started crying. Having the toilet paper nearby helped, too.

I made lists of CDs when my eyes were too tired from reading, things I wanted to buy.

I wanted to focus on being good to get the awful thoughts out of my head, but it was hard to be good. It was so hard. I had to keep my mind busy to stop thinking about it—the bridge, the drop, everything—but it was hard to keep busy when I had no real friends.

It wasn't good to buy CDs—it probably wasn't bad either, it was a pretty neutral activity—but I did it anyway, after school. I walked to Cheapo's on Bloor at Bathurst on Wednesday, when I couldn't read any more books or make any more lists or watch any more movies or drink any more of Mom's wine.

I bought the Jawbreaker album that my song was on, called *Twenty-Four Hour Revenge Therapy*, and two more CDs. I went home and listened to the Jawbreaker record over and over and over and tried to think beyond myself, about good things and good lives and people who live them. But even if I could think of something really good to do, could I do it by myself? For that I needed someone to talk to me, and it felt like no one would.

With my CDs on, I could forget about everything else around me, all the awful feelings I hadn't found a way of dealing with that were stacked one of top of each other inside me. But when I got to the last song on an album, even if I got up and hit "play" again and started from the beginning, there were still ten or thirty seconds where the problems were my own again, where I couldn't live inside the songs and make them my world anymore. Where my life was still mine. The spoiled, rich girl with a dead grandmother and a maybe-crush on someone they never wanted to be seen with.

I put Jawbreaker into my Discman and went down to the kitchen for something to eat. The only thing in the cupboard was a box of Oreos on the top shelf. I was sure my mom had put them up there, high enough so that she wouldn't be tempted to eat them. I pulled a stool up to the counter and knelt on it so I could reach the box at the top of the cupboard. I got the cookies down, unfolded the little wire clasp at the top of the bag and pulled out the plastic tray. I took three cookies out, pushed the tray back in, resealed the bag and put it back on its shelf at the top. I took a glass out of the cupboard next to it and opened the fridge, looking for a milk carton that hadn't yet expired. The only carton inside was Mom's soy milk, which I couldn't stand the chalky taste of. I settled for a glass of tap water, then reconsidered the cookies in my hand, got the bag back down and took the rest of the row up to my room. I ate them all without peeling the top cookie off and licking the remaining icing, which was how I'd always done it when I was a kid. Instead, I ate them like sandwiches, one by one until all that was left was a scattering of black crumbs on my comforter.

I walked over to the full length mirror that hung by my closet to examine myself. I stood sideways and gazed at the curve of my belly as it fell over the waistband of my jeans. I felt dumb guilt and fatness. I imagined the sweet chemicals I'd just eaten swirling around in my belly, laying soft like snowdrifts on my thighs and my butt. I chugged the glass of water I'd brought upstairs, then went back down to the kitchen and brought the rest of the bag of cookies upstairs. The CD played on repeat as I ate the Oreos row by row, standing in front of my mirror again and hating myself, and hating myself more for having given in to that stereotypical black hole of girl-body self-loathing. Once again, the story of that day ends with me falling asleep crying.

In the morning, I hid the evidence of my binge by burying the Oreo bag in the bottom of my garbage can. I couldn't see its shiny blue packaging, but I knew it was still there. I went to the bathroom and washed my face. I brushed my teeth and my hair. Put on eye shadow, mascara, eyeliner. I hadn't kept up the whole makeup routine that Megan had set out for me when we were still friends—I ditched the foundation, the lipstick—but I liked the way she'd shown me to do my eyes, even though I was using more eyeliner now than Megan ever would have advised. I got dressed and walked to school. I hoped it wouldn't show, my gluttony. Or my trip to the viaduct. I hoped that no one could tell I was still grieving in my own fucked up way. I hoped I looked normal. Maybe even good.

Marie snuck up behind me as I approached the school's front steps, and I felt a rush of relief with the force of Niagara Falls as she took my hand and walked inside with me. I was shaking. She followed me to my locker and talked as I put the books and binders I needed for my morning classes into my backpack.

"So, it's official," she said. "The band broke up."

"Oh," I said, "I'm sorry."

"Don't be. We all wanted different things and had totally different approaches to making music, you know? It was good while it lasted, but it's over. It's done. Finito. I just hope the three of us can still be friends."

"You make it sound like a break up."

"It totally was," she said. "Bands are like half-family and half-relationship. Either way, you have to work around a whole lot of different feelings and someone always ends up crying. You know, like at Thanksgiving."

"How do you know so much about this?" I asked. "Wasn't this your first band?"

"My cousin taught me a lot about playing music. She's more into metal, but she still knows her stuff and I talk to her a lot about how things have been going with the band. She's the one who had that idea about bands being like families and, like, you know, dating."

"That's cool. It must be nice having someone in your family who you can actually talk about that kind of stuff with."

"My family's great," she said. "We're all kinda nuts, so family parties are usually pretty hilarious. Oh my gosh, Christmas is my favourite. I can't believe we have to wait, like, eleven more months for it to happen again. Every year we all decorate a gingerbread house and it's, like, every year we pick a different theme. So we wind up making these crazy elaborate scenes with, like, gummy octopi and stuff, and we're singing Christmas carols out of tune the whole time, and it's just—it's great."

"Wow," I said, "that must be nice."

"I mean it's not like we're not all kind of screwed up, but we're good to each other, you know? Hey, what's wrong?"

My face had given me away. The normal was sliding off. "Nothing," I said.

"Come on," she said, "what's going on?"

I could feel the tears in my eyes a second before my face scrunched up around them, trying to shield my pathetic display.

"Oh shit," she said, "come on." And then she took my hand again, and then we were in the girls' bathroom and she was getting bunched up toilet paper from the stalls and telling me to blow my nose and wiping my face, wiping away my now-smudged makeup. My breath came in heaving spurts, and every time I tried to speak the words got strangled in my throat.

"It's-it's-it's no-nothing," I said.

"Shhh," she said, rubbing her hand up and down my back. Her hand was perfect. Her hand was good.

I could hear other girls around us opening and shutting stall doors and turning the taps off and on. "Is she okay?" one girl asked. I couldn't see who it was.

"We're fine," Marie said. "Thanks. We're fine."

Finally the bell for first period went and it was only Marie and me left in the bathroom. My crying finally calmed down to the point where I could form sentences again. I focused on her hand on my back. Up and down. Up and down.

"I-I guess I'm still sad about my grandma," I said.

"Of course," Marie said. "It's natural, of course you're sad."

"I just loved her so m-much, and she was so-so-so strong and so good. And I feel like I can't d-do anything right-right and nothing I can think of is good enough. I need t-to be good. To be, to be good. But it hurts so bad that all I can think about is-is-is—"

"Shhh," she said again, still rubbing my back. Her hand. Up and down. Up and down. "It's okay to be sad. To be frustrated. It's okay. Shhh."

And then, of course, Megan walked in to change her freaking tampon or something and she saw Marie with her arms around me, whispering in my ear with her eyes closed, and me collapsed completely into her, but with my back to the door so she couldn't see that my eyes were bloodshot from crying. And Megan started laughing this awful, high, mean laugh that I swear could only come from a cartoon super-villain.

"Ha!" she said. "What the hell are you doing? Fucking my brother was one thing, but this? This is disgusting. You freaks are made for each other."

I pulled myself out of Marie's arms and stared at Megan with nothing left in my eyes.

"I'm gonna tell everyone," she said. "You stupid queers." Then she walked back out and into the hallway and Marie and I just stood there.

"What are we going to do?" I asked.

"What do you mean," she said, "about what?"

"About Megan telling everyone that you and I are, like, gay for each other."

"I am gay," she said, "remember?"

"Yeah, but I'm not."

"So? Who cares?"

"I don't want the whole school thinking I'm—"

"What?" she said. "A dyke?"

"I'm not like you!" I said.

"It doesn't matter. It's none of their business anyway, why should you care what they think about you?"

"You wouldn't understand."

"Why not? Look, I'm not falling into this drama pit with you. You're upset enough already. The rumours don't bother me, but if anyone asks, I'll deny it if you want me to."

"That's not enough."

"Then what do you want me to do?" she asked.

"I don't know. Leave me alone."

"Fine. Have fun being miserable. You keep treating me like shit and I'm not sticking around to hold your hand any-more."

"As if that's what I want."

And I picked my backpack up off the bathroom floor and left. Wiping away more hot tears, I pushed through the school's front doors. I walked down the steps and traced my way backwards towards home.

I faked sick for the next week, which was easy since I had no one to prove it to.

I tried not to think about Marie, about her rubbing my back, about her arms around me while I blubbered and how good it felt. The whole school, or at least our whole grade, had probably all heard Megan's stupid story.

The long days at home stretched like unending roads without milestones. I drank Mom's wine and took some of her sleeping pills that I found in the bathroom cupboard to help get through the days and nights. I watched soap operas and game shows. I ate sugar cereal and jam sandwiches. I couldn't take anything off my bookshelf; I couldn't bring myself to look at any of Grandma's books. We'd finished *In the Skin of a Lion* in class. I felt like a criminal handing in an essay that was totally empty babble. I couldn't finish the book. I couldn't think about the Viaduct any more.

I was worried I might get bed sores from spending whole days in my room, so I forced myself to switch positions every hour or so. The nights were even longer than the days. The dark invited every taunt and cruelty I could imagine into bed with me, and I lay there among them until either a sleeping pill or a glass of wine knocked me out.

After a week of it, Mom finally caught on. She said she thought I needed help when she saw how many sleeping pills

I'd taken; I was so thankful she didn't notice that the wine was gone. I faked pep for a day and agreed with everything she said, while I felt my muscles pruning from lack of movement. The next Thursday she told me I had to go to school. She called a cab, watched me get in and closed the door behind me. She called out, "I love you," as we pulled out for the two-minute drive. I smiled back at her and waved.

We arrived at school, and I paid and got out. I kept my head down as I walked through the front doors and down the hallway to my locker. Possibly no one even noticed me, but it felt like every pair of eyes in the building was trained on me as I tried, once again, to look normal.

"Hey," said one of the girls in my English class who had a locker right by mine, "Mr. Grayson's been looking for you."

"Why?" I asked. "I was sick."

"We were all supposed to do our presentations on *In the Skin of a Lion* last week. I guess it's about that," she said, closing her locker.

"Okay, thanks." I got my stuff and walked to Grayson's room. Class was set to start in two minutes, and a few of my classmates had already taken their seats and were talking quietly.

"Hey, Mr. G." I was surprised to hear my own voice after my week away. "I heard you wanted to see me?"

"Katherine," he said, "glad to have you back."

"Yeah, I was really sick. Must have been the flu or some-thing."

"That might explain the, er, lack of lucidity in the paper you handed in last week. There's certainly a lot of that going around. But—no, I better talk with you after class when we have more time. Do you mind staying afterwards? I can write you a note for your next class."

"Sure," I said, "that's fine. Um, am I in trouble?"

"No," he said, "of course not. I do need you to make up your presentation mark, but I can have you do that any time, don't worry. Why don't you just take your seat now? It looks like it's just about time for us to start."

We were reading passages of *Catcher in the Rye* out loud to listen for Salinger's knack for conversational language. It was painful to listen as we each stumbled and stammered our way through what I'm sure were supposed to be such precisely chosen words. The language was just outdated enough that it all sounded, well, phony.

Then the period ended and we all packed up our things to go. I moved as slowly as I could towards Grayson's desk, fearing a line of questioning about my home life or another clichéd concerned-adult rap session. I was worried Grayson had gone ahead and made me a guidance appointment, or that he'd try to guilt me into making one myself. When everyone else had cleared out of the room, I approached his desk.

"So, what's up?" I asked.

"Oh, right," he said, "yes. The school's been given a generous donation of books, and we've been told to give them out to, well, our most promising students." He reached into the drawer of his desk and pulled out a slim, square book. "And I thought you might enjoy this." He handed it to me. "Are you familiar with Tracy-Anne Sugar?"

I glanced at the title, *Runaway Feeling*. "No," I said, "I haven't heard of her."

"See what you think," he said. "She's a young Toronto poet. I flipped through her book and I thought it might be something you'd enjoy."

"Oh. So that's it?"

"Yes," he said, "I just didn't want to single you out in front of the rest of the class."

"Okay. Well, thanks, Mr. Grayson."

"You're welcome."

"Thanks, Mr. Grayson," I said again. I unzipped my bag and put the book inside. I gave him a weak wave, opened the door and left.

I couldn't find Marie at lunch, and I wasn't sure I wanted

to. I ate in the hallway in front on my locker with the book from Grayson blocking out everything else. It was like nothing else I'd ever read. The poems sounded like someone talking to me, telling me stories about broken hearts and bad ideas. It even sounded like this person—this poet, Tracy-Anne—was talking about kissing another girl in one of her poems. Actually, she was talking about more than just kissing. I wondered if Grayson had noticed how smutty some of her poems were. My heart beat fast and I held the book close so that no one else could see what I was reading.

I practised my invisibility act for the rest of the day, and soon enough I was on my way home again. I had an email from Jack when I arrived, and I grabbed two chocolate chip granola bars from the cupboard before sitting down to read it.

> *hey kat,*
>
> *just wanted you to know i meant what i said about keeping in touch. not all us whiddens are jerks (maybe).*
>
> *j*

He'd also included a couple of links at the bottom of his message to bands he thought I'd like. It was nice. It was simple. It would be so much easier to only have relationships like this: well-intentioned, but distant. Like maybe it didn't matter that I was only half-attracted or half-interested in the guys that, on paper, I should have been crazy about. Maybe my expectations for relationships were too high. I didn't need high-stakes drama in my life, with friends and with dates. I could get used to this. I could be normal. A non-freak. I could never have sex again; it's not like I was really missing anything.

I found a scrap of paper and copied down the bands that Jack had mentioned.

I went down to the kitchen to look for something more substantial to eat than the granola bars I'd already inhaled. I found a package of spaghetti I'd forgotten we had and set a pot of water on to boil on the stove. It was rare for me to spend more than a few minutes at a time preparing anything to eat, and the water seemed to take forever to heat up. I stuck my finger into the pot to test it every few minutes until I finally saw tiny bubbles forming at the bottom. I took a handful of dried spaghetti, breaking the noodles in two with both hands, and dropped them into the pot. I took a wooden spoon out of our utensil drawer and started turning the stiff strands around in the water.

Turning my back on the stove, I went looking in the cupboard and then the fridge for something I could use for sauce.

Remembering a simple recipe Mr. Whidden had taught me once when Megan and I were hanging out at her house after school, I took a few triangles of white cheese spread wrapped in foil—substituting the rich cream cheese he had used with what we had in the fridge—and set them in a second pot with some soy milk and margarine. It didn't take long for it all to melt together. I poured the sauce over the noodles once I'd drained them and was proud to hold the only home-cooked meal I'd had in weeks in my hand.

I went back up to my room to get *Runaway Feeling* and set a place for myself at the dining room table. I'd already finished reading the book at school, but when I got to the last page I felt this insane pull to flip back to the beginning to start again. Everything this woman had written seemed right and bold and free. It was like she'd taken every word I'd been too afraid to say out loud and marked them down for me. Like a cheat sheet for my soul or something. It was kinda scary, but so, so cool.

So I sat there, reading, and eating the dinner I'd made, and felt better than I had all week. It's weird how those little pockets of almost-happy find you sometimes.

When I'd finished eating, I stuck the scrap of paper I'd written Jack's recommendations on into the book to hold my page. I took my dishes back into the kitchen, rinsed my plate and put it in the dishwasher. I considered calling Marie. I wanted to. But I didn't. The day had been boring: I'd felt spied on and ignored all at once, but there hadn't been any drama. I knew there'd be something if I called her. Instead, I went upstairs and did my homework. I finished reading *Runaway Feeling* again and went to bed early.

13

Marie was ready for me to find her the next day after school, but she didn't approach me—she waited for me to talk first.

"Hey," I said, when I saw her sitting on the front steps with her headphones on. "Hey."

"Look who's back," she said, as coldly as she could manage. It definitely wasn't her forte.

"How are you?" I asked.

"I'm great." Like she was trying to gloat, like she didn't care about me.

"Good. Good for you. I'm awful."

"I'm glad."

"And I'm sorry."

"Better."

"Really sorry."

"Better," she said again, her voice warming.

"I just—" I started to say, not knowing what would follow. "I guess I thought it was all going to turn into one of those hideous monster rumours and, I don't know, just turn everyone against us or something."

"I don't really care about why it bugged you so much. But it hurt pretty bad that you thinking that people thought we were, like, a couple was totally repulsive. Like you were judging me, or that you've just been, like, using me to go to shows."

"I'm not using—" I flinched. I *had* used her, at first. "Judging you for what—being gay?"

"Yeah."

"Jesus. I'm so sorry I made you think that. It's just that I didn't want people talking about us being... or, I guess, feeling like they had any right to know who I was and, like, who I would want to—"

"It's fine," she said, "I get it. Sort of. So are you okay with being seen with me again?"

"It isn't that I wasn't—that I didn't want to, I mean, it wasn't like that," I said.

"I was kidding."

"Right," I said, "yeah. God, can we just be friends again and drop this?"

"There is no 'dropping this,'" she said. "But yeah, I think we sort of need each other right now."

174

"Thanks for being the one who gave a shit."

"You're welcome."

"So," I said after we'd stood in silence for a little while, trying to get over ourselves. "Any big shows this weekend?"

"Oh wow," she said, "haven't you heard? Josie from Falter's playing solo Sunday night at Holy Joe's."

And just like that we were back to normal. It was such an unbelievable relief.

"How would I have heard?" I said, "I only get this stuff from you."

"Of course, that's the real reason why you need me." I flinched again, but she was kidding this time. "Your social planner extraordinaire, your conduit to the musical underbelly of the city—c'est moi."

"Yeah, haha. Are you serious, though? About Josie? I'd love to see her play on her own."

"Good, so you'll come with me?"

"Yes," I said. "I'd love to."

Agreeing to the show meant I was totally screwed, again. Marie—sweet as she was, good to me as she could be—only brought more drama with her. I wanted so badly to see Josie again: to see just her, to sit and let my eyes and my brain and every part of me be taken up by her voice and her face and her everything else.

The stupid thing was that I almost loved Marie. Even when I was hiding from the rumours that we were a couple, I kept having dreams about her. I imagined us playing in a band together, opening up for Falter and Royal Pain. I pictured getting her drunk and comforting her as she sobbed about breaking edge. I wanted to change her the way I could feel her changing me.

I thought about how she would know how to be good, that we could do it together, maybe. But then we'd talk or she'd yell my name—or I'd even just remember her yelling my name or doing something too loud, doing something she wasn't supposed to—and I'd lose that feeling. So I figured that I couldn't be in love with her after all, if I wanted to change everything about her. Not that I knew anything about it, but I was pretty sure that wasn't how love was supposed to work.

But being with guys was so simple. So much more simple. It didn't mean changing the entire way you thought about yourself, had always thought about yourself. You were just you with a boyfriend—or, just you, but with a bunch of guys who were friends and who talked about simple things and technical things and didn't make your heart hurt every two seconds.

With Marie, with Megan, with Jacque and Macy, there was so much going on at every level of conversation. I don't think any of us really even knew we were doing it, but even when Megan and I hugged each other and told each other we were best friends, some part of me was jealous that her dad was always home when we got there; he was such a good cook and he told funny jokes sometimes, and mostly he cared and he was there. Meanwhile, Megan was hugging me back and probably hating me because Mom had gotten a raise at the station and I bought the new pair of jeans that cost more money than she got for allowance in a year. But it wasn't just dads and money, it was everything. There was so much to care about that it hurt. It sounds dumb to say, but it was so damn hard to be a girl.

I read more Tracy-Anne Sugar—I'd found another one of her books of poetry in the school's library—and I cooked dinner again Friday night, listening to Jawbreaker and the new Eric's Trip CD I'd bought. I thought about the outfits Marie and I would wear in our fantasy band: looking tough, but still approachable and sweet. In the fantasy, I was taller and my jeans didn't fit so tight around the waist. I thought about taking her hand after the last song and kissing it in this fantastic, chivalrous way. Then I thought about Megan taunting us, pictured her standing at the front of the stage with her tongue stuck out between her second and third fingers. I thought about Josie, and I ran a bath.

Mom was home on Saturday, and she said it was time that we sort through Grandma's things. "I can't believe we've put it off like this," she said, "but I've just been so busy at work." She'd gone down to the retirement home not long after Grandma died to supervise some men she'd hired to pack everything up, but the things had been in a storage space since then. She'd borrowed a van from work and we drove out to the space to sort out what to keep, what to throw away and what to give to our relatives.

"I'm glad we're doing this together," she said as we pulled off of our street and onto Bloor. "I hope this won't be too hard for you."

"It feels weird to be digging through her stuff,"

"Yes, honey, but we have to do it. It's all been sitting in that storage locker too long already. But we're in this together, right?"

"Sure," I said.

And it was weird going through all of Grandma's old stuff—her art, the paintings and prints that had hung on her walls for so many years. My parents took those. She had tonnes of jewellery, pieces that had come from all over the world. My mom made me pick out a few things, and the rest we put into bags to give to my cousins and aunts. I already had most of her books. Her sight had deteriorated a lot in the last few years, and I remember her taking me aside one day and telling me to take whatever I thought I would read from her shelves. "I can't read any of them anymore," she said. And it wasn't in a self-pitying way, it was totally matter-of-fact, but even her being so matter-of-fact about it kind of killed me. I took the books, though. They were all I wanted of her things.

It took us a few hours to go through it all, but not as many as I thought it would. That an entire life could be reduced to the contents of a storage locker was so gut-punchingly depressing that I almost cried about a dozen times. I didn't, though. I was starting to wonder if I'd already run through my tear quota for the year. And it was only the beginning of February.

We carried loads of her things to and from the car until the locker was empty and the van was piled with things that were no longer hers. Mom went to the main office to settle up with the owner of the space, and I sat in the passenger seat of the van, rubbing my dry eyes. She came back smiling, but in a way that I knew meant she was forcing herself to keep it together in front of me.

"It's okay," I said. "You don't have to. Hold it in, I mean." And we sat there, looking at each other with watery eyes, for a few minutes before Mom finally turned on the radio to snap us out of it. She put on the oldies station and started singing along. I joined in feebly on the choruses I knew, and we rode like that all the way back.

Dad was home when we got there, and the three of us sat in the living room together for a while without saying very much. We were sort of on a roll, family-wise—unbelievably rare for us—so Mom suggested we go out, catch a movie and maybe have some dinner.

It's something that families do all the time, I guess. Spend time together. Normal families. But, apart from the funeral, I couldn't remember the last time that the three of us had done something all together. None of us knows how to act in normal family situations, and it always feels like we're playing pretend.

And, on top of it all, seeing my dad after his many unexplained nights away from home, which Mom still hadn't called him out on, made me want to scream.

I knew that Grandma would have told me to cut my parents some slack—advice she'd given me more than once when I'd arrived at her house, furious over one childhood injustice or another, begging her to adopt me. She would have sat me down and explained that my mom and dad were under a lot of pressure, but it didn't mean that they loved me any less. That I had to be patient with them, even if they weren't always patient with me.

Grandma would have told me to go to the movie. She probably would have told me to be less suspicious of my dad, too. She would have told me a lot of things; she would have kept me balanced, sane.

I had to learn to do that for myself now.

So I agreed to go along.

Besides, it's not as if I had anything else to do.

We looked up what was playing at the Cumberland Theatre and figured that we'd find somewhere to eat afterwards in Yorkville, an upscale neighbourhood that apparently used to be totally radical in the '60s.

"A late, great family dinner in the old stomping grounds," Dad said. I pulled a sour face. Dad likes bragging about his former hippie days once in a while, but the stories never change. He never seems to notice people nodding in that we've-heard-this-one-before kind of way.

The day had turned out to be warmer than anyone had expected, so Mom suggested we walk to the theatre. Dad acquiesced and put on the one pair of running shoes he owned, the ones he saved for his infrequent trips to the gym. Mom locked the front door, Dad took her hand and we started walking. I let them walk ahead, while I followed behind—leaving enough distance that it wouldn't be immediately clear that I was with them.

After ten minutes or so, when they'd run out of things to say to each other, Mom dropped Dad's hand and called back to me, "Honey, come up here and walk with us."

Dad was acting sickeningly normal. Like he was trying to cover his tracks by playing the part of the Average Joe Family Man. It's not that I wanted to expect the worst about my dad, but I had such little idea of who he really was as a person that when he started spending so much time away from us, I just assumed that he was having an affair. But maybe he wasn't, maybe he was just tired of being a husband and a father and just wanted some time to himself. I was sure that I'd never know, that with no one honest left in the family this was going to be our new normal. But the fact that Mom was going along with it made it even worse.

I breathed in deep and tried to think of Grandma. This sane and balanced act wasn't working well so far.

"No thanks," I said, "I like it back here."

Dad chuckled and said, "Of course, she doesn't want to be seen with old folks like us."

Mom got kind of pissed when he said that, and the two of them argued the rest of the way there. I counted my steps on the sidewalk and tried to keep my mind blank as we walked.

I kept imagining throwing daggers at their backs. Tried to banish the thought.

Sanity, balance, nothingness.

Daggers.

I counted more steps.

When we got to the theatre, there was a short lineup at the box office. I saw that Megan and Pat were at the front of the line buying tickets, and I cringed when I overheard her say the name of the movie we were seeing, the one that Mom had chosen. I was glad my parents were still bickering, because it meant Mom didn't see Megan, so she didn't try to say hi. Pat and Megan got their tickets, paid and then went to go line up for popcorn. By the time we'd gotten to the front of the ticket line, they'd already taken the escalator upstairs without noticing us. Mom paid for our tickets and the three of us headed for the escalator. We found our theatre, which was dark already and mostly full, on the next floor, and I couldn't see Megan or Pat inside. We chose seats near the back, and I excused myself to go to the bathroom before the trailers ended and the movie began.

I went down the stairs to the women's washroom, but

stopped when I saw Pat standing outside the doors, presumably waiting for Megan. I cursed under my breath—feeling stupid for being such a coward—and went back to the theatre. A few minutes later, as the movie was just about to start, Mom saw Megan with Pat walking down the aisle to find a pair of seats.

"Megan," Mom whispered in a way that sounded more like a shout. "How are you? Why don't you two come sit with us?"

Megan paused for a second and looked at the three of us. I held my breath and waited for venom. But she didn't say anything. She just took Pat's hand and kept walking.

As they walked away from us, Mom whispered, a bit quieter this time, "That was Megan, wasn't it, honey?"

"Yeah," I said, "that's her."

The movie was all right, but seeing Megan there had pretty much ruined it for me. She was all I could think about, even with the actors in the film projected larger than life on the screen. I kept replaying her laugh from when she walked in on Marie and me hugging in the bathroom that day. It was like that laugh blocked out every good memory I had so that all that remained was the feeling of being a freak on display, being completely cut off from everything I thought

I had been, and everything I'd been when Megan and I were still friends.

The lights came up as the credits rolled and I unzipped my purse, pretending to look for something I needed but couldn't find, keeping my head down. Megan and Pat slowly extricated themselves from each one another, picked up their garbage and started to walk out of the theatre. I stared into my bag, rummaging for something I knew didn't exist until I was sure they'd left the theatre.

"Is everything okay?" Mom asked.

"Can we just sit here for another minute?" I said. "I don't really want to go out there right now."

"Because of Megan?" Dad asked. "I hate to see you fighting with your best friend. The Whiddens have always been so good to you."

"Dad? Drop it, okay. You have no idea what's going on with me."

"Now hold on," he said, "I know I'm not around as much as I'd like to be, but it hurts to hear you say that. I'm still your dad. You're still my little girl, even if you're not so little anymore."

"Is that a line from a movie or something?" I asked. "Do you even know what you're saying?"

"If I knew it was going to be melodrama night, I wouldn't have come along," he said.

"Great," I said, "then I think our wholesome family time is officially over."

"Oh, both of you, stop it," Mom said. "Let's pick somewhere to go for dinner."

"I'm not hungry," I said.

"Neither am I," said Dad.

"Henry, you're coming to dinner with me," Mom said. "Katherine, I'd like you to come, too, but I can't force you."

"I just need to take a walk and clear my head I think," I said. "This Megan stuff is too hard to explain."

"Are you sure?" she asked. "Your dad and I are great listeners." I almost laughed at that. It was the biggest lie I'd ever heard.

"No," I said, "I don't want to talk about it. You guys go, have date night. I'm going home."

We got up from our seats and left the theatre. My mom hugged me by the exit doors; they turned right and I turned left.

I didn't feel like going home right away, and I really was hungry. I went into the McDonald's nearby, across the street from the museum, where I used to always bug my parents to take me for lunch after our educational weekend trips to see the mummies, the bat cave and the dinosaur bones. I ordered Chicken McNuggets, a box of ten, and sat down to eat them. I got through eight before I started feeling sick. The fatty, salty crunch I remembered wasn't the same, but I finished them anyway, dunking them into two little tubs of sweet and sour sauce. Afterwards, I felt bloated and gross and sat there for a few minutes staring at the grease stains at the bottom of my cardboard McNugget box, thoroughly repulsed.

From there I walked home. I dragged my heels through the thin layer of snow that had fallen on the sidewalk and looked at the people I passed. They all seemed to be holding hands, every single one, even though I knew that was, like, mathematically impossible. Everyone looked so content and fulfilled, like even if they had problems in their lives they weren't so big that they couldn't be solved. They looked like they all had people they could really talk to about their problems, people who would listen and hold them and just be there with them. And I dragged my grease belly along, feeling ugly and stupid and unloved and not good enough to deserve anything better anyway. It was pathetic and I knew it, but it didn't change the way I felt.

Back at home, the house was still. I climbed the stairs to my room and lay down on my bed. I got the magic, cursed fifty out of my wallet and held it above me, studying it. I tried to pretend that it didn't bother me that I couldn't come up with something good to do with the money. Money could only do good, I was convinced, if you had an unending supply. And even then it was more likely to make you miserable than happy. Growing up, money had never been an issue. It was always there when we needed it, and even though my family didn't spend like crazy, we still had a lot, a lot more than other people I knew. But it didn't make any of us happier. It was this awful, all-powerful thing that drove the whole world around—trying to make it, trying to keep it—but it didn't really do us any good, as far as I could see. Which was easy for me to say, of course. I'd always been the Rich Girl. So it was all meaningless, and I'd finally figured that out, but who cared about some spoiled, fat, sad, maybe-gay princess' opinion anyway?

Definitely not Mackenzie King, whose face was as impenetrable as always. He stared through me—his thin smile belittling me, tormenting me—until the paper burned in my hands and I had to put him back in my wallet so he'd stop looking at me.

14

Then it was Sunday. Mom and Dad had gotten home late
the night before, after I'd already fallen asleep. It seemed like
they'd somehow managed to salvage a decent evening out of
our movie-going disaster. I almost wished that I'd been there
to watch it happen, since their love for each other was like an
imaginary friend: easy to talk about, but impossible to see.

Maybe Dad hadn't been cheating after all. Or maybe
Mom was willing to overlook it. Whatever had happened, I
knew they weren't going to tell me. It was just another missing piece of the puzzle.

It was great for them—and our family's fighting chance at
normality—this bizarre appearance of affection. But the fact
that they'd been able to have a good time after I left made me
feel like I was the one messing our family up.

They were in the kitchen together when I woke up, at
around eleven. Dad already dressed, Mom still in her bath-

robe. They were drinking coffee and reading the newspaper. They looked like a couple who might actually love each other, but they didn't really look like parents. I said a quick good morning, and told them I'd had a nice quiet night on my own and that I was feeling fine. I poured myself a giant bowl of Froot Loops and added milk, which, miraculously, had actually come from a cow. Dad must have picked some up some time yesterday.

"You sure you wouldn't prefer some pancakes?" Mom asked.

"Since when do you make pancakes?" I asked.

"I can make them when they come out of a box."

"No thanks," I said, "cereal's fine. I have a date with Toucan Sam."

I spent most of the day doing my schoolwork and waiting for Marie to phone me about the concert that night. I thought maybe I should just call her and make a plan for the show, but I didn't quite feel up to it, and besides, I knew she'd call me. I played *Ms. Boatman's Wild Ride* a few times over in my old Walkman and picked out what clothes I was going to wear that night. By eight o'clock, when I still hadn't heard from Marie, I started wondering if something had happened to her. I opened my agenda to where I'd written her number and was just about to start dialling when the phone rang. I picked it up.

"Hey," Marie said, "Kath? Kathy? You there?"

"Yeah," I said, "hey."

"Sorry I didn't call sooner," she said. "I was talking to Chantal—you remember her, right? My friend we hung out with at Falter last time? Well anyway, Chantal's in the middle of this major drama-fest because she told Ivan she was still in love with him, and I think she was maybe kind of jealous that you guys had kissed that night, you remember, but she said Ivan said he doesn't like her that way. And she was freaking out because they'd promised to go see Josie's show together, but she doesn't want to go with him, but she has to because she promised. Honestly, it's kind of a headache. And from what you said, this guy is a total waste-of-space creep."

"Worse."

"Yeah, he's an asshole. But they've got, like, history or whatever. She wouldn't listen when I told her what a jerk he was with you. She's being really weird. Normally she's cool, but Ivan seems to bring out the crazy in her. It's exhausting.

"Anyway, Macy and I hung out yesterday and jammed a bit, just the two of us, but then I guess she told Jacque about it and now Jacque's pissed at me even though she pretty much quit the band and, I don't know, everything's just kind of sucky and weird right now and I kind of hate everyone, you know? I'm feeling really overwhelmed."

"Yeah," I said, "I know the feeling. But do you still want to go see Josie tonight?"

"Are you kidding? The thought of seeing her play is, like, the only thing keeping me sane right now. You're still in, right?"

"Definitely, I really want to see her. Do you want to meet at Bathurst in an hour?"

"That sounds perfect," she said. "Totally perfect. I'll see you then."

I put my copy of *Runaway Feeling* into my purse so I'd remember to bring it with me. The book was an amulet, it was my protector. It was sacred, it was holy.

We met up and rode the streetcar south. Marie didn't say much, she just sat there resting her head on my shoulder, and for once I didn't squirm away or tell her to stop goofing off. I just focused on her weight resting on me, holding me down and keeping me grounded. We got off at Queen and walked over to the Big Bop.

"So it's the second door, right? The Reverb door?" I asked.

"You bet," said Marie, walking past the Kathedral's double doors to the Reverb's smaller door and holding it open for me. We climbed the stairs to the second floor. "We're going upstairs," Marie said to the girl working door at the Reverb. "To see Josie from Falter's show at Holy Joe's."

"Fine," said the door girl, and she let us walk past.

I followed Marie past the Reverb's bar, which ran along the back of the room, past the bathrooms and the small hallway to the stairs she'd pointed out to me the first time we were here. The stairs opened into a small front room at the top, where we paid the five dollar cover and had our hands stamped. The front room opened into one that was slightly larger, about the size of a large basement, with couches lined up along the walls and Christmas lights hanging from the ceiling. We found an empty couch at the front of the room—there was no stage, but there was a space cleared at the front that was obviously where Josie would be performing very, very soon—and parked ourselves. We'd only just settled in and taken off our big coats when Marie saw Chantal and Ivan come in. She waved at them and they came over to join us.

"Hi, guys," Marie said, "it's nice to see you. I can't wait to hear Josie; can you imagine how amazing she must be when there's no band behind her to distract you? Ah-mazing!"

"Yeah," Chantal said, "I can't wait. Isn't that her over there?" She pointed to a tall woman leaning over to talk to the sound guy at his booth.

"Stop pointing," I said, "she'll see us."

"Isn't that the whole point of a show this small?" Chantal said.

"Yeah, I guess," I said, "but we don't want to look like geeks."

We'd all failed to notice Marie get up from the couch when Chantal had pointed Josie out. We failed to notice, that is, until we saw her approach Josie, tap her on the shoulder and, when Josie turned around, give her a hug. I was completely in awe. Josie didn't look freaked out at all. She kept laughing and touching Marie's shoulder, tilting her head to the side and clicking her big boots together. They looked like old friends, maybe even girlfriends, and my face flashed hot with jealousy.

"Oh man, is Josie a dyke?" Ivan asked.

"I think she's, like, bi," Chantal said.

"That's kind of hot," he said.

"I have to go to the bathroom," I said. I got up and went downstairs to the Reverb's bathrooms—Holy Joe's didn't have its own—picked a stall and sat down. What did it mean to feel like this about Josie and Marie? It didn't mean anything, the two of them talking like that, it was just the rock star-groupie dynamic. Josie couldn't honestly care about Marie. She was so much older and in such a cool band. They were just starting to get some airtime on the Edge, the big rock radio station in town, and their music video was playing on Much Music all the time and Josie was obviously going to be a star. And Marie wasn't even pretty, really, not in a conventional way like Josie. She was just, like, so obsessive that you had to just give in and be sucked into her gravitational pull. She made you feel important. But she couldn't do that for Josie, how could she?

I sat there, thinking and trying to figure it all out, reading and rereading parts of *Runaway Feeling*, until someone rapped on the door. I yelled out, "Occupied," and the girl on the other end of the door said, "Yeah? Well none of the rest of these flush, so hurry up!" So I pulled up my pants and kicked the toilet plunger. I washed my hands without soap— the dispensers were empty—wiped my hands on my jeans and walked back upstairs.

Josie was up at the front tuning her acoustic guitar, and Marie was sitting on the couch next to Chantal and Ivan. I took my spot back beside her and she squeezed my arm.

"Can you believe this?" she whispered. "Josie's so cool. I was just talking to her and you have no idea how cool and down to earth she is. It's amazing, it's totally incredible. Oh wow, I hope she plays 'Stray Dog.'"

"What did you guys talk about?" I asked. "Was she, like,

weirded out that you just came over and talked to her?"

"What? No, not at all. She remembered me from that Falter show a couple of weeks ago, can you believe that?"

"Wow," I said. "Wow. That's great."

And then Josie's guitar was all tuned up, I guess, because she started to play. And there were only maybe thirty people in the room, but it seemed like she was singing to every person individually. She played some songs she said were new, a couple that were Falter songs and a few that she said she didn't know where they'd end up, that maybe they were just for her—and for us, since she was sharing them. And they were so beautiful, and she was so strong and lovely.

She was talented and she was sharing her talent, using it to make other people feel and understand the world the way she saw it. And she gave a damn. She was nice to Marie and so sweet on stage with her little bits of banter between songs. She was exactly where she wanted to be: with her guitar in her lap, perched on a high stool. She was so good. But I was still afraid she might actually have a crush on Marie.

After her set, we all sat around talking for a little bit while Josie packed up her guitar and Marie said she was working up the courage to ask for her phone number. Any time I looked at Ivan, Chantal gave me a weird hands-off look, so I didn't talk to either of them and said I had to go get a glass of water from the bar. Marie took that as her cue to tackle Josie. As I got back to the couch, glass in hand, I saw Josie scribble something out on a piece of paper, hand it to Marie and kiss her on the cheek, then walk over to a group of her friends, some of whom I recognized as members of Falter.

"You really got her number?" I asked Marie, who looked about ready to swoon when she came back to where we were sitting.

"I know!" she said. "Isn't it amazing? Do you think I might actually have a shot with her?"

"No," I said.

"She's hot," said Ivan. "If you're not going to call her, I'll totally take her number."

"That's gross," Chantal said, "she's obviously into Marie."

"I don't know," I said. "You're so much younger than she is. She probably just thinks you're a cute little fan girl."

"She's only twenty-five," Marie said. "That's only, what— seven years difference? My stepdad's seven years older than my mom."

"That's totally different," I said.

"I think it's cool," Chantal said. "Good for you. Let's just hope it goes better than the last time you fell for an older girl. That university chick totally smashed your heart, didn't she?"

"I got over it," said Marie.

"I'm just saying," I said, "I think it's kind of weird."

"What's your problem?" Marie asked.

"Nothing," I said. "Nothing. Can we go now?"

"Aren't there, like, other acts playing?" Chantal asked.

"Whatever," I said, "I saw what I needed to see. I'm going."

"Me too," said Ivan.

"Well, whatever, I'm going to stick around," Chantal said. "See you guys later."

So Ivan, Marie and I walked out together, and Ivan was trying to talk me into taking the streetcar home with him, which was, like, the last thing I wanted to do. And I was surprised he still had any interest in me given how things had gone down the last time, but it seemed like he'd been drinking again, so Marie and I walked him to the streetcar stop and I told him we were going a different way. We said goodbye and he tried to hug me, but I moved out of the way and instead he stumbled and nearly fell off the curb and into the street.

As we watched the streetcar doors close and the car roll off, Marie said, "So really, what the hell is going on with you?"

"Nothing," I said, "it's really nothing."

"Shut up with that," she said, "why are you acting so weird about me hitting on Josie? Are you really just that worried about me dating an older girl? Because I've done it before, it's no big deal. Like, age really isn't this big thing we make it out to be. If you think about how everyone learns in their own time, and how we're all socialized differently and every-thing and—"

And half because I'd been dreaming about doing it non-stop for, like, weeks, and half because I wanted to shut her up, I kissed her. Right there on the sidewalk. I kissed her, and she kissed me back. For a second, anyway.

"Whoa," she said, pulling away, "I thought we were just friends."

"We are," I said. "I just—I just wanted to see."

"I didn't think you liked me that way. You never seemed to."

"I do, sort of," I said.

"This is weird," she said. "This is a bad idea. I'm getting you a cab." She flagged one down and put me in it. "You'll thank me for this later," she said, closing the cab door.

I turned around in my seat and watched through the back window while she got smaller and smaller as we drove away. I put my hand inside my purse and felt the sacred book. It hadn't done shit to protect me. I put it on my shelf when I got home. It was stupid to think that a book could save your life.

The next day was Monday, and I wanted to skip but I couldn't stand the idea of spending the whole day by myself. Even facing Marie would be better than watching daytime TV and stuffing my face with junk food and then hating myself for it. Drama class had become even more of a joke since Mr. Neilson's breakdown, and I had a spare second period, but even thinking about sitting around the house in my underwear depressed me, and somehow school seemed like the more forgiving option.

I got dressed, took an apple out of the fridge—strangely enough, Mom had bought groceries the day before—and walked to school. Marie was waiting at my locker when I arrived.

"Hey," she said, "how are you?"

"The real answer?" I asked, avoiding her eyes, her intense stare.

"Okay, I get it. I wanted to talk to you about last night so you understand why I did what I did. I mean, it isn't that I wasn't totally flattered. The kiss was unexpected, yeah, but it was sweet. But I don't think this is what's best for us. I think we need to just be friends, okay?"

"Yeah," I said. "You're—I mean it wasn't exactly premeditated, but I get that you don't think we, that we wouldn't be good—"

"We're friends," Marie said. "Can we agree to each be the one drama-free spot in each others' lives? I mean, not that you're not allowed to have drama, you know, but just not to drive each other crazy?"

And just a second before I opened my mouth to speak, it occurred to me how unbelievably lucky I was that Marie had put up with me and still seemed to like me, that she trusted me, somehow, and wanted us to have the kind of friendship that makes both people feel loved and good. At least that's how it felt in that moment.

"Yeah," I said, "that would be good. I think I need that right now." And we hugged again, this time without tears.

When I got home that night, I sat down at the computer to send Jack an email since I still hadn't replied to his message.

> *hey j,*
>
> *nice to hear from you. i bought an eric's trip cd on your suggestion. you were right, i love them.*

And then I couldn't think of what else to write. It seemed simple enough, and maybe it was easier to keep the message light, to not really say anything. Jack existed in a grey area of trust. Still, he'd reached out to me. He tried to care and to be good. Better late than never, right?

> *also (and it feels kind of weird for me to type this out, but I think I need to, so here goes):*
>
> *i think i might be gay.*

I highlighted what I'd just typed with my cursor and hit "delete." Then I typed it out again, just as I had before. Then I hit "send." After that, I just sat there for a while. It was the best I'd felt in a really long time.

15

The next couple of weeks, things weren't great, but they were better than they'd been. Marie and I met up every day before school to trade CDs and gossip about her almost-nightly phone calls with Josie. Macy sometimes hung out with us, too, though mostly she hung out with her drama club friends, and it was just me and Marie.

I felt good when we were together—like I was able to be totally myself, whichever version of myself I was that day—and I tried hard to keep from being jealous when she told me about her conversations with Josie.

"She's even more amazing now that I've gotten to know her," Marie said one day. "It's like, admittedly, I had this little fan girl crush on her before I really knew her, and I was more into her image and stuff than who she is as a person. But she's so amazingly relaxed and real, you know? She even told me about some of her exes—guys and girls. She's actually really sweet when she talks about them. Like she knows those relationships ended for a reason, but she still respects what they meant to her, which is, like, so refreshing compared to all this high school drama, you know?"

"Speaking of which," I said, "how's Chantal doing?"

"Well, she was sort of upset that you kissed me that night after we all hung out."

"What, you told her? Why the hell does she care who I kiss?"

"Yeah, sorry about that. It just sort of came up. She was complaining about how she thought you were flirting with Ivan that night—"

"Flirting? I barely even talked to him."

"She's definitely the jealous type," Marie said. "Anyway, I only told her that you kissed me so she'd know you weren't into Ivan."

"What, so now Chantal thinks I'm a slut? She was the one with the shirt that actually said *SLUT* the night I met her."

"Forget about that," she said. "Remember? We're beyond all this dumb high school stuff now. A few more months and we'll be out of here completely."

I took a deep breath in mock meditation, and we both started giggling. "Come on," I said, "we better get to chem."

A week or so after I'd sent my email to Jack, I got a reply. I hated admitting to myself how anxious I was to hear what he had to say. He was the last person I'd expected to tell, but I'd sent the email anyway. Pressing "send," it'd felt so definitive.

I think I might be gay.

It felt weird, though, kinda like I'd confided in the wrong Whidden. But making up with Megan definitely wasn't an option, and I needed to, well, maybe not shout it from the rooftops, but at least send the message out to someone I'd known a long time. And every time I thought of Megan, I couldn't get her mean laugh out of my head.

Jack's reply was short.

hey kat,

glad you're into eric's trip. they're definitely the coolest thing to come out of moncton pretty much ever.
i was surprised by your message, but I feel kind of flattered (honoured?) that you chose to tell me. do your parents know?

j

I thought about playing it cool and taking a day or two to write back, but I was too excited to wait.

> hey jack,
>
> eric's trip are from moncton? my mom was born there, small world.
> i haven't told my parents yet. i think i'm going to wait until i move out for university.
> thanks for being decent (i mean that in a good way)
>
> kat

I only got one more email from Jack, a couple of days later. He kept it brief.

> always happy to be decent.
>
> you should check out fifth column. they were a toronto band from the 80s. played crazy experimental punk stuff. plus i think most of them were gay. queercore, check it out.
>
> j

Which was somehow exactly what I needed to hear.

Things were starting to settle back into a rhythm that passed for normal, even though I'd picked my life up, shaken it and put it down again in a different place than it'd been before—snow globe style, or something.

School dragged on, but it was manageable. I got accepted to all the schools I applied for, and Marie and I talked about maybe being roommates somewhere, we hadn't picked where. She said Concordia, I said Dalhousie. I didn't know how serious either of us was, but it was nice to be able to talk like that. Like good friends.

I still thought about the fifty. I couldn't believe I'd let it just sit in my wallet for so long, let Mac King mock me every time I opened it to get change for the Coke machine. I hadn't even told anyone about the money. I'm sure everyone at school would think I was crazy. They'd tell me to spend it on beer, or maybe weed, to have a good time and live up the little time we had left in school before getting shoved out into the real world, or something like it. But there had to be something I could do with it. There had to be something.

Marie was still totally obsessed with Josie. They'd finally met up for coffee one day after school and they'd wound up going for dinner—Pad Thai at Java House—because they'd been having such a good time.

"I know she's older than I am and everything, but really, I hardly notice the difference. And she doesn't drink! Did I tell you that? She said she's made enough dumb decisions while she's been drunk that's she's quit now, for good she says. Which is so great because it means she thinks it's cool that I'm straight edge, which is, like, so rare, you know? I don't know, I don't think she's into me yet, but she likes me and we really get along. I think she could be into me. I think we could be great together."

"That's really cool," I said, "I'm happy for you."

And I was happy. Even though the wanting was still there, wanting Marie so bad it was all I could do to keep from kissing her again. I only felt it sometimes; half-sure I'd imagined it, like a stone in my shoe.

I sat in on one of Marie and Macy's jams a few days later. With just two guitars there was only so much they could do together, but it sounded great—folkier than before, dreamier. Macy's voice was beautiful and you could hear it a lot more clearly without Jacque's heavy-handed drumming over top. It still sounded punk—if that's what you could call the noise they'd been making with Jacque—but it was more grounded and earthy. I was amazed.

"You guys sound awesome," I said when they took a break between songs to re-tune. "Really, I like how simple it is with just the two of you. You should totally just be a band on your own."

"You think?" Marie asked. "Because finding another drummer would be such a pain in the butt. You really don't think we need one?"

"I think you should probably make sure Jacque's not plotting to kill you guys," I said, "but yeah, I think this is it. I think this is the way the band's supposed to be. Now all you need is a name."

"There's a few we've talked about," Macy said. "Trippers was one."

"Which is like 'trippers,' like people who fall a lot," Marie said, "which is kind of like Falter so we decided not to use it. Plus it sounds kind of like a stoner name."

"What was the other one?" I asked.

"Mother Night," Marie said, "because I saw the name on a book—it's by Kurt Vonnegut, I think—and thought it sounded good, but, you know, I've never actually read the book so we figured that wasn't a good choice. I think there was one more, though. Macy, do you remember?"

"The Kims," she said. "We thought that was kind of clever. You know, like how we talked about Kim Gordon and Kim Deal?"

"But it's not quite right," Marie said. "Everyone will expect us to be, like, Korean."

"We'll think of something," Macy said.

They packed up their guitars. We ordered a pizza and ate it while watching *Wayne's World*, which we'd all seen about a million times each.

"I think I'm going to ask Josie if we can open for her at her next solo show," Marie said, wiping cheese grease off her chin.

"That would be so cool," Macy said.

"Yeah," Marie said, "I'll ask her tonight. No—no, wait, I'm going to call her right now."

Before Macy or I could protest, Marie had grabbed the phone sitting on a nearby table and dialled Josie's number, which she apparently knew by heart.

"Hey, Josie?" she said.

Silence. We couldn't hear Josie's end of the conversation.

"Yeah, it's me again. How are you, how's your day been?"

Silence.

"Oh, that sucks. Bummer. But you've got to practise, right? Don't you guys have a show coming up?"

Silence.

"No, I'm sure it'll be great. Seriously, you guys kill every time."

Silence.

"Totally. But look, I was wondering, do you guys need, like, an opening band for your St. Catherine's date?"

Silence.

"Oh, okay. Well what about something in town, some other time?"

Silence.

"No, we're good, we're totally ready. My friend Kathy sat in on practice today and she said it sounded great."

Silence.

"We're uh... we're called Dream Woman. We're a two-piece now. It's sort of more folky. We actually thought it would be so great to open for you at one of your solo shows."

Silence.

"Oh, okay, that's cool."

Silence.

"Sure, I'll talk to you soon."

Silence.

"Yeah, bye."

Marie hung up and Macy looked at her all concerned. "Is everything okay?" she asked.

"Kind of," Marie said. "Man, I feel so dumb."

"What happened?" I asked.

"Well, like she wasn't mean about it or anything," Marie

said, "but I could just tell from the way she asked about the band—oh, man, I actually thought she might've liked me! But I was so wrong. She thinks she's, like, my freaking big sister or something. This really sucks, this is so stupid. I feel like such an idiot."

"No," Macy said, "no. I'm sure it's not like that. Maybe she was just really tired or something."

"I'm a total idiot!" Marie said. "All those nights I stayed up so late just to talk to her and I could barely wake up for school the next day, they were a waste, a total waste. And, oh man, now I can pretty much never go to a Falter show again. Dammit! Why do I always do this?"

"Whoa," I said, "geez, calm down. What did she say exactly?"

"That she was tired. That her boss was being a jerk. That she had band practice. That they were playing a show soon in St. Catherine's but that the booker's a total sleaze and she can't stand him. That they already have bands to open for them there. That she doesn't think we'd be ready to open up for Falter. That she didn't think she was going to play any more solo shows. And that she had to go."

"So she's under a lot of stress," I said. "That's normal."

"No," Marie said, "I heard it. I heard it in her voice. It's like I'm a pesky little bug to her. She hates me."

"I doubt that," Macy said.

"Well neither of you know anything about it," Marie said. "Can you both just go now? Please? I need to be alone."

"Are you sure?" I asked. "I think you're making a big deal out of nothing."

"No," she said. "Get out of here. I'll see you guys at sc-school tomorrow." Marie started sniffling and I knew she was about to cry. So we left, and that was it for band practice.

Macy and I were each headed home in a different direction, but we decided—almost without speaking—to walk to the subway together so we could talk about Marie.

"I'm really worried about her," Macy said. "I've seen her get really hung up on stuff like this before; she takes it pretty hard. Like with this university girl last spring? She got her heart broken and then moped around for months. It was awful. And now I'm worried that this Josie situation is going to be like the spring all over again."

"Seriously. Just watching her face sink while she and Josie were on the phone was, like, torture."

"I know. We should do something for her. You know, to cheer her up."

"Yeah," I said, "that's a great idea. Like buy her a little present or whatever, like something for the band maybe."

"Totally. We've got to get her focused on the good stuff

that's happening. So what do you think she'd like?"

"I don't know," I said, trying to think of what their pretty, folky new sound could use. I tried to remember the sounds of Dad's old records, the ones he used to bring up from the basement once every few years when he'd start waxing nostalgic about his hippie days in Yorkville. Which I was never quite able to figure out. How could my father, the most uptight, business-like man in the world, have been some guitar-strumming, flower child freak? Though I guess it means I come by my freakdom honestly, which is almost sort of comforting. It's also kinda weird that Yorkville used to be the dirt-cheapest neighbourhood in the city—at least that's what my parents say—and now it's the ritziest; not a dirty hippie in sight.

"We can't get her a guitar, that'd be too much money," Macy said. "Ha, maybe we should get her a tuner. It always takes her forever to tune by ear, you know?"

"That might be the wrong message for a cheer-up present," I said. "You guys need something to, like, help bring out this new sound. Like, I don't know, a banjo, or a fiddle or something. Something that'll be fun for Marie to mess around with while her heart's, uh, mending. A harmonica maybe? A ukelele?"

"A ukelele? That's totally perfect! She'd love that."

214

"Great," I said as we arrived at Lansdowne station, and I fumbled with my wallet, looking for change for the subway. "Uh, how much do you think a ukelele's gonna cost?"

Macy paused, thinking.

"We could probably get a cheap one for, I don't know, fifty bucks?" she said.

And then everything made sense. Everything, the whole stupid world. It was perfect. I could do the good and get the girl all at once. It was perfect. It was good.

"That's-that's great," I said. "There's a music store near Ossington station, right? I'll stop in on my way home and, uh, see what they've got."

"Excellent," Macy said, "I knew you'd think of something."

Macy knew I'd think of something. Somehow, I'd become the kind of person who other people—people who'd been relative strangers up until recently—thought could think of things. Important things. I smiled. Macy put her token in the collector's booth, and I dropped in my handful of change: six quarters, three dimes and four nickles. She gave me a hug, and we said goodbye. I took the stairs down the westbound subway, and she took the ones for the eastbound train.

Down on the platform, Macy and I could still see each other, separated by two sets of subway tracks. We were too far to talk, so we just smiled at each other, and Macy waved at me while we waited. Her train arrived first. She got on, found a seat and then waved again as her train pulled out of the station.

I unzipped my backpack and pulled out my wallet. I tried not to go around waving my money in the air, but I was too excited to keep this to myself. The answer to everything, to honouring Grandma, and maybe even believing in love, and doing something good—really good—for a friend and maybe more. I could hardly believe this stupid, red piece of paper was the answer to it all, but it was. It was. It was.

I stood just at the lip of the platform, my feet toeing the edge, so that the people behind me couldn't really see what I was doing. I took out the red bill, the fifty, the bully Mackenzie King, from my wallet. I held it up in my left hand and kissed it. I noticed a man looking at me from a little ways down the platform, looking suspicious and predatory. He yelled at me in this fast, barking way, and I turned around because I couldn't hear what he'd said and he totally startled me out of my perfect little dreamy bubble world, and I watched outside of myself in super-slow motion as my fingers opened, just a little, tiny bit, and I dropped the fifty. I saw my right arm stretch out in front of me to grab the money, but I was too late. The bill fluttered down below the platform and onto the subway tracks. And it lay there, crimson against the dark of the tracks. My last hope.

I panicked. My pulse started beating a million drum rolls. I felt sweat dripping down the back of my neck. My mouth tasted like dust and blood. Mac fucking King stared back up at me, his cold little eyes and smug expression dared me to do it.

Because, I mean, this was it, this was the only chance I had to make everything right. This was the only thing that was going to bring me and Marie together and make me feel okay about us, the two of us, together. It was the only thing that was going to make me feel okay about Grandma, too, and maybe even Megan. And I didn't see the train coming, I swear I didn't. I thought I could jump down fast enough to get the money and then climb back up. I really thought I could.

So I jumped down onto the tracks. And that's when I saw the headlights coming towards me. The train.

The police officers who were called to the scene gave me a ride home. The one who was driving dropped me off at my front door and said, "Take care of yourself, all right? You better not do anything this stupid ever again. Okay?"

I mumbled, "Okay," and let the officer riding in the passenger side walk me to the door.

Mom answered the doorbell looking totally shocked, but that could have just been because she's mortified of being seen without her makeup on by anyone other than me and Dad.

"Your daughter did a very dangerous thing today," the police officer said to my mom. "But she's all right now." Then, turning to me she said, "Now go on, get inside."

I walked on newborn fawn legs to the living room, where I collapsed onto the couch. My mom stood talking to the police woman for a few more minutes, then came inside and sat down next to me.

"I can't believe that," she said. "I can't believe you'd do something like that. I had no idea things were this bad. Honey, I'm so sorry. I had-I had no idea. I'm so sorry." She hugged me, and I let her.

"Mom, it's not what you think," I said, wiggling out of her vice-like grip. "Really. I wasn't trying to—you know. I wasn't, I swear."

"Well," she sniffed hard, "even if you weren't, I still feel so, so badly that I haven't been around more lately. And I'm sure all of this isn't just about your grandma, and I understand that you're never going to tell me what's really going on, but I need to know that you're going to be okay. And I'm going to—I'll make some more time and, well, try to be around here more, all right? I'm going to try a little harder to be your mother. Okay, honey?"

"Yeah right," I said. She had me tearing up, too, so I fought back with sarcasm. "Who are you again? The maid?"

"I'd hope the maid might vacuum the carpets once a year, wouldn't you?"

And we laughed. We actually laughed, together, even though we were still crying.

So Mom went ahead and made some promises about

how she was going to take some time off of work to try and be around more. Dad, too. She said she'd talk to him about spending more time at home. Doing more stuff as a family.

I wanted to believe her, so I pretended I did.

We talked about finding someone for me to talk to, a professional. A shrink or a therapist or whatever. I said I'd give it a try as long as she didn't make me go see the guidance counsellor at school. That woman was totally awful. I figured if I was going to be getting help I'd better make sure it was the good stuff—not just inspirational posters and pamphlets on eating disorders. It was time for something real.

We hugged again.

And she actually felt like my mother.

It would have been really nice if Dad had been home. To tie the story up, to clear up everything we'd left unsaid. He wasn't there, though.

But it was still pretty nice.

The next day was Friday. I couldn't believe how long the week had been. It wasn't enough to find the answer to all the world's problems and then to have to face your death, apparently. You still had to go to chemistry class.

I got there early, hoping Marie and I could talk before class, but the minutes ticked past and she didn't show up. Ms. Dixon shut the door and started the lesson, but Marie didn't come screeching in late, either. The period ended, and I put my books and binder away, and she didn't come.

I called her house from a pay phone in the front foyer after school, and after, like, eight hundred rings, Marie finally picked up.

"Hey," I said, "where are you?"

"What do you mean?" she said, "I'm at home. How else could you be calling me?"

"I know, but why aren't you here? You know, at school? How come you didn't show up today?"

"I wasn't exactly up for it. I've been taking a mental health day."

"What, by listening to Falter all day long?"

There was a shamed pause. "I listened to Jawbreaker, too."

"I'm coming over, okay?" I said. "I'll be there in half an hour."

"No," she said, "you can't. The house is awful right now, it's so messy. And I look like I've been crying all day."

"That's a look I'm pretty familiar with."

"You really want to come over?"

"Yes," I said, "I really do."

"Fine," she said. "I'll see you in half an hour."

I walked toward Bathurst station, but I couldn't go inside. I could still remember the stink of the tracks and the perfect darkness underneath the platform. I could still hear the train. I figured I could probably get to Marie's house on foot soon enough if I walked fast, so I kept going west on Bloor toward Lansdowne, the browny-grey slush slorping around my boots as I walked.

I arrived out of breath from my little power-walk and knocked three or four times on the door. Then, realizing that Marie had a doorbell, I rang it several times for good measure.

Marie answered the door in pyjama pants with cartoon sheep on them and an oversized Falter T-shirt. Her eyes were very, very red. "Cuhmon nin," she said, her nose stuffed up. She pulled a Kleenex out of the pocket of her pyjamas and blew hard before putting it back in her pants.

We went up to her bedroom and she sank back into her bed, where it was obvious she had spent most of the day. I sat down next to her on the rumpled sheets.

"This can't all be about Josie," I said. "It's not that bad, is it?"

Marie blew her nose again and then spoke.

"I fall for this amazingly perfect person, someone who I

think might like me as much as I like them, and I spend all this time with them and go totally crazy about it, and then it turns out that they don't care about me at all. It's horrible. It hurts so much."

"There'll be other people," I said, "you know, fish in the sea and all that."

"I don't eat fish."

"I don't think that's what that expression is about."

"Whatever, leave me alone."

"You remember when I told you that?" I asked.

"Yes, duh."

"And I didn't really mean it."

"Yes, duh."

"So you don't really mean it."

"Fine, whatever."

"Hey," I said, "you didn't even ask me what I did last night."

"Okay," she said, with feigned enthusiasm, "what did you do last night?"

So I told Marie all about the train and the money, though I was careful to avoid mentioning what the money was supposed to be for.

"What?" she said. "No way, that's insane! That's so, so scary! I can't believe you let me go on and on about—when you almost died!"

"Yeah, I still can't believe it happened. It was... it was really scary."

"Oh my god." She put her arms around me and it felt good. Good-good. "Why did you care so much about the money anyway?" she asked. "Isn't your family, like, loaded or whatever? No offence."

"No," I said, "none taken. It's stupid. But I-I found that money right after my grandmother died and I, well, I decided that I had to do something good with it. And Macy and I were so upset about how broken up you were about Josie that we decided we should get you a little present to, you know, cheer you up."

"So that money was for me?" She dropped her arms.

"I was going to buy you a ukelele."

"That's the dumbest thing I've ever heard."

"What do you mean?" I said.

"You almost got killed so you could buy me a baby guitar to make me smile?"

"Uh, yeah. Sort of. Pretty much." I breathed in hard through my nose. I was going to have to say it fast or I'd never get up the nerve again. "The thing is that I kind of love you, and I wanted you to get over Josie because I think it's stupid that you're so worked up over some dumb, million

225

year-old guitarist who happens to have amazing style and is also really, really nice, because she doesn't know you like I do, not really, and I just want you to be happy. You're so good to me. You're so... good."

Marie looked at me. She blinked. She kept on looking. She wasn't smiling. Finally, she spoke, "The thing is that you kind of what?"

"I know you think that we're better as friends, but I think that-that I've just been so confused and sad this whole time, but I'm neither of those things when I'm with you. I'm just, I'm just good."

"Since when has being good been so important to you?"

"I don't know, it's just some theory I had." I was being rejected; my speech slowed, I tried hard not to cry. "Like, I don't know, just, like, an idea."

"It wasn't Josie I was so upset about," Marie said, her voice hardly louder than a whisper.

"What?" I said.

"I said it wasn't Josie. Josie was just, I mean, I like Josie a lot. And I did have a crush on her. I kinda still do, to be honest. But I was thinking today that it was stupid to be this upset over someone I didn't in all honesty, really, you know, believe I could be with. And I figured out I was so upset because of you."

"What do you mean?"

"Like I've been holding it all in or something, you know, the real rejection. I guess I, I don't know, tried to put you out of my head. Turns out my head's not such a big place after all."

"It's... you..." I said.

"Yeah, for a while now."

"It's me."

"Yeah," she said, "it's you."

Wow.

Wow. Wow. Wow.

"Get dressed," I said, "we've got somewhere to be."

"Where are we going?" Marie asked.

"We're going to buy you a ukelele."

"That's the dumbest thing I've ever heard."

And then we kissed again.

And neither of us pulled away.

And it was good.

AUTHOR'S NOTE

While most of this book is as faithful a recreation of Toronto at the turn of the millennium as I could manage without some form of time machine, a few of the details were just plain made up. More specifically, while many of the bands and authors referenced in the story are living, breathing, fabulous artists, a few of them are homages, amalgamations and otherwise not real (yet). Among the fake bands are XgloryX, Daydream Nationalists, Falter, Stark, Royal Pain, and TEAM (though that's a bit of an inside joke—TEAM was my band in high school).

I found my own Tracy-Anne Sugar, and I hope that you will, too.

ACKNOWLEDGEMENTS

Thank you, thank you, thank you to my incredibly supportive family who have in no way provided the necessary angst for me to ever become a successful writer. Mom, Dad, Sam—I love you guys. One more time: thank you.

This book was produced with the support of the City of Toronto through the Toronto Arts Council, and for that I am thankful.

This book was also produced with the support of Sheila Baird through an envelope that turned up in my mailbox at exactly the right time, and for that I am even more thankful.

To the writing groups I've been fortunate enough to be a part of—the Dewdbury Group and the Flaky Lushes—thank you for telling me when the words were good and when they weren't. Sometimes it really is hard to tell.

Demian Carynnyk was an early cheerleader for this story back when it still featured a talking dollar bill as a central character and was called *The Boat Dream From The Hill*. (I know, right?)

I picked *The Boat* to pieces in Amy Deverell's living room. And, because I probably won't win the Giller any time soon, I'll have to thank the Deverell-Gavigan-Andrews household here.

If I say that I don't have enough space to thank the rest of my friends by name it makes me sound conceited, doesn't it? Special mention to the Posse, the Gang, and the Book Citizens.

Sarah Wayne and Brendan Ouellette deserve nothing but kittens and sunshine forever for all of their hard work in making this thing you're holding in your hands (or reading on your preferred electronic device).

And to Graham Christian, who never failed to be ridiculously supportive when I shirked social obligations (and sometimes bathing) to get the book ready for print. It was an awfully nice thing to do.

SUZANNE SUTHERLAND is a Toronto-based writer, former bookseller, and editorial assistant in children's publishing. Her short fiction has appeared in various magazines and literary journals such as *Descant*, *The Rusty Toque* and *Steel Bananas*, and she is the co-founder of the Toronto Zine Library. This is her first book.

Follow her on Twitter: @sutherlandsuz